by John Updike

———

POETRY
THE CARPENTERED HEN (*1958*)
TELEPHONE POLES (*1963*)
MIDPOINT (*1969*)

NOVELS
THE POORHOUSE FAIR (*1959*)
RABBIT, RUN (*1960*)
THE CENTAUR (*1963*)
OF THE FARM (*1965*)
COUPLES (*1968*)
RABBIT REDUX (*1971*)
A MONTH OF SUNDAYS (*1975*)
MARRY ME (*1976*)

SHORT STORIES
THE SAME DOOR (*1959*)
PIGEON FEATHERS (*1962*)
OLINGER STORIES: *A Selection* (*1964*)
THE MUSIC SCHOOL (*1966*)
BECH: A BOOK (*1970*)
MUSEUMS AND WOMEN (*1972*)

ESSAYS
ASSORTED PROSE (*1965*)
PICKED-UP PIECES (*1975*)

PLAY
BUCHANAN DYING (*1974*)

FOR CHILDREN
THE MAGIC FLUTE (*1962*)
THE RING (*1964*)
A CHILD'S CALENDAR (*1965*)
BOTTOM'S DREAM (*1969*)

THE
POORHOUSE
FAIR

John Updike

THE POORHOUSE FAIR

With an introduction by the author

Alfred • A • Knopf • New York

1977

THIS IS A BORZOI BOOK
PUBLISHED BY ALFRED A. KNOPF, INC.

Acknowledgement is made to Penguin Limited,
for permission to quote from Luke 23:31 of E. V. Rieu's
THE FOUR GOSPELS.

Library of Congress Cataloging in Publication Data
Updike, John.
The poorhouse fair.
I. Title.
PZ4.U64PO8   [PS3751.P4]   813'.5'4   76–21156
ISBN 0–394–41050–5

Manufactured in the United States of America
Published January 12, 1959
New Edition published February 1977

If they do this when the wood is green,
what will happen when the wood is dry?

INTRODUCTION
TO THE 1977 EDITION

THE PRESENT is the future of the past. Driving back into Boston the other night, I looked across the river at the not especially spectacular skyline of East Cambridge and saw it as a nineteenth-century man might have seen it: as parabolic and luminous splendor continuously and coolly on fire, as pyramids piled of cubes of light, each high-rise apartment building a gigantic perforated lantern twinned in the black river and crowding the sky with golden outpourings of energy. Even the glowing advertising signs—FOOD FAIR, ELECTRONIC CORPORATION OF AMERICA—appeared magnificent, unaccountable, authoritative in their strangeness. Who had set such a marvel here? Only a race of gods, it seemed, could inhabit and power this ribbon of the future unrolling on the far shore of the Charles. I was amazed, an alien.

Twenty years before I had stood by a low wall in Shillington, my birthplace in Pennsylvania, and looked down at the razed acres where for all of my boyhood the poorhouse had been. I have described it elsewhere:

At the end of our street there was the County Home—an immense yellow poorhouse, set among . . . orchards and lawns, surrounded by a sandstone wall that was low enough on one side for a child to climb easily, but that on the other side offered a drop of twenty or thirty feet, enough to kill you if you fell. Why this should have been, why the poorhouse grounds should have been so deeply recessed on the Philadelphia Avenue side, puzzles me now. . . . But at the time it seemed perfectly natural, a dreadful pit of space congruent with the pit of time into which the old people (who could be seen circling silently in the shade of the trees whose very tops were below my feet) had been plunged by some mystery that would never touch me. That I too would come to their condition was as unbelievable as that I would really fall and break my neck.*

Now the poorhouse was gone. Out of the hole where it had been, there came to me the desire to write a futuristic novel in commemoration of the fairs that I had attended here as a child.

Backward time, forward time carve the same abyss. The novel of the future seeks to give us in concentrated form the taste of time that flavors all novels, that makes their events more portentous than the events of our lives, where time passes unnoticed, but for the rare shudder, and the mechanical schedule. With superb and dreadful poetry H. G. Wells' *Time Machine* moved its hero through time so fast that he "saw the sun hopping swiftly across the sky, leaping it every minute, and every minute marking a day"; upon acceleration "the palpitation of night and day merged

---

* *Assorted Prose*, 1965, p. 156.

into one continuous greyness" and "the jerking sun became a streak of fire, a brilliant arch, in space." The sun, simultaneous symbol of life and of its transience, is visited by the Time Traveller on the verge of its own extinction, when it hangs in the sky "red and very large, halted motionless upon the horizon, a vast dome glowing with a dull heat." He pushes thirty million years further on, to when "the huge red-hot dome of the sun had come to obscure nearly a tenth part of the darkling heavens." It is bitterly cold. The sea is blood-red and tideless. The sole signs of life are green slime and a vague creature out on a sandbank—"it was a round thing, the size of a football perhaps, or, it may be, bigger, and tentacles trailed down from it; it seemed black against the weltering blood-red water, and it was hopping fitfully about." How horrifyingly real, to my thirteen-year-old imagination, was that animated-cartoonish survivor (oblong in my mind like an American football, instead of round like an English one) at the end of the world. The vision could not be dismissed; it was a nightmare that, as would my own death, *would come to pass.*

The totalitarian nightmare of *Nineteen Eighty-Four*, like the Eloi/Morlocks class war of Wells' fable, would *not* come to pass, at least in the United States: so it seemed to this patriotic adolescent. Reading Orwell's novel in my late teens, I was titillated by its anti-Soviet allegory; but the book developed a claw of iron when O'Brien, Big Brother's spokesman (and a cousin perhaps of my Conner), told the captive hero:

"You must stop imagining that posterity will vindicate you, Winston. Posterity will never hear of you. You will be lifted clean out from the stream of history. We shall turn you into gas and pour you into the stratosphere.

Nothing will remain of you: not a name in a register, not a memory in a living brain. You will be annihilated in the past as well as in the future. You will never have existed."

Orwell knew he was dying as he wrote that terrible imprecation; personal dread drove him to touch futurism's black center: the death of everything. The ultimate fruit of the future is non-existence. Not only our egos but all their memorials and progeny are swallowed by the sun's bloating, by the stars' slowing, by entropy. Congealed of gas, we return to gas. In Huxley's *Brave New World*, which I read at a still later, admittedly less impressionable age, deaths occur, but without immensity. The Savage's suicide at the end is mockingly objectified, trivialized even: the corpse's dangling feet, slowly twirling, give the directions of the compass. As in our mundane reality it is others that die, while an attenuated silly sort of life bubbles decadently on. This is, one could say, the vision of the future offered in *The Poorhouse Fair*.

The novel was written in 1957, as a deliberate anti–*Nineteen Eighty-Four*. Its events, I asserted in the solicitous flap copy that was then left off the first printing, occurred "about twenty years from now"— that is, now, twenty years later. The pre-dating was done with some accidental imprecision. John Hook, the hero, is ninety-four; in the first pages he remembers himself freshly graduated from normal school in "the fat Taft's administration." Taft was President from 1909 to 1913; assuming that normal school in Hook's day meant a two-year post-high-school curriculum, he would be twenty years old upon graduation, which would put his birth between 1889 and 1893, and the time of my novel right around 1984. But I wanted it to fall short of that year, as its political ambiance fell short of *Nineteen Eighty-Four*'s dire absolutism; in the Modern Library edition (now out of print) I amended the administration to "the first Roosevelt's," Taft's's predecessor. TR's ample reign (1901–1909) places my future's near rim in the late months of 1975 (McKinley was assassinated in September of 1901) and is amply congruent with the novel's other muddled checkpoint (p. 84), the anniversary of the St. Lawrence Seaway, whose opening in 1959 was itself in the haze of the future when I pinned my novel to it. At first I had the anniversary "silver," the twenty-fifth, which again nudges 1984; for the Modern Library I altered this to "crystal," which, as the fifteenth, places it *too* near; "china," the twentieth anniversary, is about right, though it sounds brittle. But the entire editorial, as a piece of prediction, lives up to its quaint style.

How do they match up, the world of *The Poorhouse Fair* and the world that surrounds us now? As long ago as 1964 it seemed necessary to say, in a brief foreword to the Modern Library edition, that

I meant the future it portrays to be less a predictive blueprint than a caricature of contemporary decadence. Though I expected that some details would be rendered obsolete, I did not imagine that Hook's rhetorical question . . . "Isn't it significant, now, that of the three presidents assassinated, all were Re-publican?" might abruptly become impossible. I have let it stand, as a vivid anachronism. I thought, in 1957, fondly composing this latter version of the stoning of St. Stephen, that the future did not radically differ from the past; and this notion now seems itself a product of the entropic years of the Eisenhower lull.

Not only was John Kennedy assassinated in the twenty years prior to 1977, but another President resigned, and the Vietnam Involvement escalated and collapsed, and with it a wave of civil dissent such as has not been seen in this country since the Civil War. It is hard to know what Hook refers to when he says, on page 152, that "This last decade has witnessed the end of the world, if the people would but wake to it." He cannot be referring to the Arab oil boycott and the rising squeeze on raw materials, for the automobiles that come to the poorhouse seem to be still of Fifties dimensions, and the poorhouse furniture has a reassuring ring of solid stuff, of brass and rubber and frosted glass; the tags on the porch chairs are sturdy metal, and simple "soybean plastics" represent our throwaway multitude of synthetic polymers. Nor can Hook be thinking of the global realignments that place the Soviet bloc with the "have" nations and turn Russia and China to enemies and encourage our own surprising rapprochement with the red dragon, for Truman is still remembered as the President who "gave away China to the Russians." Something called the "London Pacts with the Eurasian Soviet"—a bow, it may be, to *Nineteen Eighty-Four*'s division of the planet into Eurasia, Eastasia, and Oceania—dominates the peace wherein American population soars "like diffident India's." Our population no longer soars, as it turns out. *The Poorhouse Fair* foresees widespread voyeurism but not the pornography boom; its popular culture has a wrong Hispanic accent, but the brown tint seems right. The romantic vanities of Ted the truck-driver and Conner the youthful poorhouse prefect savor more of a Forties boyhood than of our guarded, unenthusiastic Seventies. The characters reflect back through the riots and revolts of the Sixties as if they had never occurred—and so, to an extent, do we. There is a present truth in the sentence, "The nation became one of pleasure-seekers; the people continued to live as cells of a body do in the coffin, for the conception 'America' had died in their skulls." There are striking technological omissions: where are the computers, and the Xerox machines? Buddy should be using an electric typewriter, and can his typing table really be porcelain? Drugs, so much in our news and so prominent in *Brave New World*, figure only as a dose of flavored penicillin exclaimed over as a novelty by an anonymous fairgoer. An even stranger absence is that of television, crucial in Orwell's scheme of tyranny and the present-day mainstay, the continuous electronic *soma*, of nursing homes and retirement villages. Nothing is quainter about my old people than their never seeming to watch television, and their having to fall back for entertainment upon reminiscence and mischief. But, if the next seven years bear me out, I was right where Orwell was wrong: no atom bombs have fallen, and the governmental forms of the major western democracies have not succumbed to Big Brother. In 1977 Hook continues his inward walk down a "long smooth gallery hung with the portraits of presidents of the United States," though a President Lowenstein has not been one of them.

The main flaw of my "predictive blueprint" inheres in any attempt to predict the course of multiple and intercausative phenomena such as make up the life of a nation or a planet. We can extend the graph curve of present trends and be certain that existent vitalities will decline, but we cannot conceive of the new, of the entities born by intricate synthesis from collisions of the broadly known. Models of the future tend therefore to be streamlined models of the present, the present with its corners cut off. But it is these very corners that move into the center and become the future. They move unexpectedly and perhaps unpredictably, even to the supreme intelligence hypothesized by Laplace, who said, "nothing would be uncertain for such an intelligence, and the future like the past would be present to its eyes." Determinist faith in essential predictability has been challenged, recently, by David Layzer, who, deploying the laws of thermodynamics and the concept of phase space, concludes that "not even the ultimate computer—the universe itself—ever contains enough information to completely specify its own future states. The present moment always contains an element of genuine novelty and the future is never wholly predictable."* It is such a future, an unpredictable one wreathed in mists as of nostalgia, a fuzzy old-fashioned non-future of a future, that I tried to render in this novel, imitating not the science-fiction classics mentioned above but the obscure poetic *Concluding*, by Henry Green. *The Poorhouse Fair* shares with *Concluding* an embarrassing number of particulars: an old estate housing a vague State-run institution (a girls' school, in Green's case), a not-too-distant time-to-come (fifty-five years hence, *Concluding*'s jacket flap stated in 1948), an elderly monosyllabic hero (Mr. Rock), a multileveled action drifting through one day's time, a holiday (Green's fête, Founder's Day, even falls, like the poorhouse fair, on

---

* "The Arrow of Time," *Scientific American*, December 1975, pp. 56–69.

a Wednesday), heraldic animals, much meteorological detail, and a willful impressionist style.

—Old and deaf, half blind, Mr. Rock said about himself, the air raw in his throat. Nevertheless he saw plain how Ted was not ringed in by fog. For the goose posed staring, head to one side, with a single eye, straight past the house, up into the fog bank which had made all daylight deaf beneath, and beyond which, at some clear height, Mr. Rock knew now there must be a flight of birds fast winging,—Ted knows where, he thought.

That is from Green's first page; this is from mine:

In the cool wash of early sun the individual strands of osier compounding the chairs stood out sharply; arched like separate serpents springing up and turning again into the knit of the wickerwork. An unusual glint of metal pierced the lenient wall of Hook's eyes and struck into his brain, which urged his body closer, to inspect.

The innocently bold eclecticism of my youth rouses my envy now. A million or more published words later, my sentences are less purely mine than these stolen from Green, with their winsome inversions confident as a child's speech ("With the eye it was not difficult to follow the shining squares all the way down the line") and their soft straining to combine sensual "touch" and subjective mythifying ("Despite the low orange sun, still wet from its dawning, crescents of mist like the webs of tent caterpillars adhered in the crotches of the hills").

The novel, reread, seems best when it deals with John Hook and at its weakest with Conner; the antagonists rotate the novel in and out of credibility. Conner, in his thirties, was too young for me to understand; what goes on in his cupola I guessed at as I guessed at what went on in the principal's office of my high school. ("A principle is a ru*le*," the spelling teachers used to tell us, "but the principal is your *pal*.") A nervous self-conscious shyness, and maneuvering around that shyness, dominate Conner and Buddy as if they were adolescents. Conner is a high-school goodie-goodie, trying to make his way among sardonic rowdies, tied by pious ambition to invisible grown-ups —invisible like the grown-ups in *Peanuts*, like the human beings in Kafka's "Investigations of a Dog." He should have been more. Whereas Hook's antiquity shrinks him to the scope of my still basically childish imagination. His physical and visual impairments impose the same magical discontinuities that a child's handicaps of perspective and ability do. Like a child he is in love with the world and hopes that the world loves him. He is alert for clues, though blind to patterns. His perceptual style controls the book; the parakeet, the rabbit on the lawn, the "silver zeppelins" of Lucas's pigs (there are swine in Green, too) are seized upon with relief, as something alive but intelligible, by the presiding, animistic imagination. The flap copy went:

Animals haunt the landscape, and inanimate objects—a sandstone wall, a row of horsechestnut trees, a pile of pebbles—strain wordlessly toward the humans, who act out their quarrels of tradition versus progress, benevolence versus pride, on a ground riddled with omens and over-borne by a massive, variable sky. The author seems to separate sense and existence; the chatter of the mob that comes to the fair in its sense illustrates the national decay that obsesses the pensioners, yet in its existence, isolated by bits in the air, shares with grass and stones a positive, even cheering, *anima*.

There is, then, a philosophical ambition here; an attempt, no less, to present the meaning of being alive, as

conveyed by its sensations. Our eager innate life, re-
bounding from the exterior world, affirms itself, and
the quality of affirmation is taken to be extrinsic, im-
manent, divine. I needed God to exist. My claim that
the banal American chatter that dissolves the novel at
the end manifests "a positive, even cheering, *anima*" is
a leap of aesthetic faith sheerly—a child's delight in
being up late, eating licorice while grown-up conversations make a sky of safety above his head, recalled
fifteen years later and forcibly assigned a clinching
position in an argument sketched, I see now, along
Thomist lines. Like a Thomist proof the novel moves
from proposition to objections to counter-objections.
The distinction between essence and being (*essentia*
and *ens*) I took from St. Thomas; with his help I
sought to consecrate, to baptize into American religi-
osity, those three very atheistical Englishmen, Wells,
Orwell, and Henry Green. The original manuscript
ended a page sooner, upon the Chestertonian lament
"to guard the gates of the deserted kingdom." Small
wonder the ending baffled what were to have been the
book's publishers; good luck or Providence led me to
an editor, Stewart Richardson, and a publisher, Alfred
A. Knopf, who to my lasting gratitude printed this
book in a format as exquisite as my intentions, my text
unaltered.

That was twenty years ago. Now I notice, in this
text, amid the religious schemata, a less conscious
pattern, announced by the sentence already quoted,
about the strands of osier arching like separate serpents
springing up and turning again into the knit of the
wickerwork. The image forced itself upon me at the
outset of the action; it returns on page 27, as Hook

: **xviii** :

remembers himself as a child examining his bedcovers, "searching for the deeper-dyed thread that occasionally, in the old woven cloth, would arch above the others." This microcosmic event is dramatically enlarged when, amid the schoolyard rumpus of the stoning, Hook, studying the interwoven clouds of the sky, has "his narrow field of vision crossed by a flow of arrowing stones, speeding through the air in swift flocks, and before he considered, he had the thought that here was something glorious. Battles of old had swayed beneath such a canopy of missiles" (p. 132). The hurled stones arch; and so the entire incident itself arches up out of the fabric of the day, and then is turned again into the knit of the gossip that ends the day. Buddy carries the scandal into the crowd (p. 172) and composes a comic headline in the air (p. 176); by page 180, amid the threads of several other rumored scandals, the event is anonymously made to yield a moral ("you sometimes need a man with a look of authority") and allowed to fade from the common discourse.

The people who had come to the fair talked more slowly, tending toward affectionate gossip about the past they had in common as citizens of the town, and about roads and schools and old houses sold. Coarsened hands of still handsome women nervously tucked back stray strands of hair; young mothers pouted under the weight of sleeping babies.

Ipswich has displaced Shillington behind this evocation. The Massachusetts town where I wrote this novel, in the three summer months of our first year there, has begun to intrude upon the remembered town; young mothers and sleeping babies join my cast of characters.

Life goes on; stray strands are tucked back; the stoning has sprung up and been turned again into the knit. All is flux; nothing lastingly matters. Such pessimism came more naturally to the author of *The Poorhouse Fair* than his hopeful detection of a world-soul. For me, the most surprising—the most abruptly *given* —image occurs on the penultimate page; the stars are perceived as "not specks but needles of light suspended point downward in a black depth of stiff jelly." Earlier (p. 39), Hook, praying, had felt his mind as "a point within an infinitely thick blanket." We are *within*, the young author feels, honestly claustrophobic— within a universe where the sun daily grows "orange, oblate, and distended"* and then plunges to its death like some Titanic deity. For a while the furrow plowed by its plunge glows "the color of an unnatural element, transuranic, created atom by atom in the scientist's laboratory, at inestimable expense" but, as the sick-ward patients watch, clouds propelled by evening winds obscure the golden chasm. The poorhouse is fair, I wanted to say, against my suspicions that it is, our universe, a poor house for us.

The book was published early in 1959. Wright Morris and Mary McCarthy found kind words to say of it, and Mary Ellen Chase published in the *Herald Tribune* a review of extraordinary enthusiasm and warmth. Others found it precious, for all the "phenomenal composure" of the prose. *Time*, after what I took to be a panning, cited it among "The Year's Best" and

---

* Cf., of course, the sun at the end of *The Time Machine*. And, of the stars, this sentence by Wells may have been in my memory: "The circling of the stars, growing slower and slower, had given place to creeping points of light."

I had the pleasure of seeing myself anointed, in their regal way, "Gifted Writer Updike." *The Poorhouse Fair* arched back smoothly into the vast knit of past seasons' books. It sold about eight thousand copies, and has been kept in print by the publisher's generous policy in this regard. This is its sixth printing; the fifth was in 1966. A few lingering typographical mistakes have been cleared up, the historical clues have been adjusted as mentioned above, Gregg's expression "a.h." has been liberalized to "a.hole" (though I am pleased with my solution, for those days, to the problem of printed obscenities; better my abbreviations than non-words like "fug" or eye-catching dashes), and what appears to be the same boy at the fair has been given the same name throughout, Mark. Otherwise the text is unchanged; I could not write this novel now, and will respect the man who could. He wanted to lay down in these theorems and raptures the foundation for a tower of volumes, its title a slogan to prosper by. A few days ago I submitted the manuscript for my twentieth book. The future is now; it is as if, standing by that poorhouse wall, I threw myself down, into the pit of time, and, my neck unbroken, find myself here.

JOHN UPDIKE
Boston, Mass.

THE
POORHOUSE
FAIR

I

"WHAT'S THIS?"

"What's what?"

"Why, *look*."

In the cool wash of early sun the individual strands of osier compounding the chairs stood out sharply; arched like separate serpents springing up and turning again into the knit of the wickerwork. An unusual glint of metal pierced the lenient wall of Hook's eyes and struck into his brain, which urged his body closer, to inspect. Onto the left arm of the chair that was customarily his in the row that lined the men's porch the authorities had fixed a metal tab, perhaps one inch by two, bearing MR, printed, plus, in ink, his latter name. A reflex of pride twitched the corners of his mouth; he had always preferred, in the days when certain honors were allowed him, to have his name spelled in full, with the dignity of the middle initial: John F. Hook. On the adjoining chair the name of his companion, Gregg, was similarly imposed. With the eye it was not difficult to follow the shining squares all the way down the line.

"What birdbrain scheme is this now of Conner's?" Gregg asked noisily, as if the taller man might not hear. "Is he putting tags on us so we can be trucked off to the slaughterhouse?"

"Well, yes: what is it? A child must tinker."

"They'll come right off," Gregg said and produced from the hip pocket of his shapeless wool trousers a black bone jackknife of the old style, with a blade for removing the metal cap from bottles. With this blunt blade he adroitly began to loosen, not his own nameplate, but Hook's.

Gregg's small brown hands, the thumbs double-jointed and spatulate and the backs covered with dark lines as fine as hair, sought leverage with a quickness that recalled to Hook that his companion had been, before alcohol and progress had undone him, an electrician.

"Here," Hook said, hoarse as much from the discomfort it caused him to focus his eyes on action so near at hand as from disapproval. In truth he felt helpless. He enjoyed no real control over Gregg, though some crooked whim or weakness led the younger man lately to cling close to Hook's presence. It was Hook's misfortune to have the appearance of authority yet lack the gift of command. He sought a reason that would stay Gregg. "If we forget our place, they'll take the chairs themselves off, and we'll be left to stand."

"And then all die of heart attacks; I hope we do. It'll make a f.ing black mark in Conner's book, to have us all keel over without a place to sit."

"It's a sin to talk on so," Hook exclaimed positively, for death, to his schoolteacher's mind, was a bell that must find the students with their noses to the desks. "And," he went on, "it is a mis-take for the old to mo-lest others' property. The young now, the young have nothing, and may be winked at when they steal a foretaste; but those who have had what there is to be had are expected to be beyond such foolishness. We fellas so close to the Line"—he raised his voice on this last word, inclined his head, and lifted his right hand in a dainty gesture, the index and little fingers pointing upward and the two between curled down—"have our accounts watched very close." The disciplinarian's instinct—which was somewhat developed, though he had always lacked the cruelty to be the disciplinarian paramount—told him these words had been correct for the purpose; he had a shadowy sense that what Gregg sought in his company were elevated forms of thought to shape and justify the confused rage he felt toward the world that had in the end discarded him. Also, there was something in the relationship of Hook's teaching the younger man how to be old; Hook at ninety-four had been old a third of his life, whereas Gregg, just seventy, had barely begun.

"Ah, we can pick them off with our fingers any time we want," Gregg said with contempt, and, nimbly as a monkey on a rubber tire in the old-fashioned zoos, he turned and sat in Hook's chair, rather than the one labelled as his own.

"Modern day workmen are not what they were,"

Hook stated, satisfied. Standing on one porch edge, he rested his gaze in the comfortable depths to the east and north of the porch: shallowly concave farm plains tilled in scientifically irregular patches, the nearer lands belonging to the jurisdiction of the Poor Home; further off, small hills typical of New Jersey; presiding above, a ribbed sky, pink, betokening rain. The blurred click of Gregg's blades being snapped back into the sheath satisfied him still further. Pain ebbed from the muscles of his eyeballs as they lengthened to suit the horizon, and he felt positive pleasure. Despite the low orange sun, still wet from its dawning, crescents of mist like the webs of tent caterpillars adhered in the crotches of the hills. Preternaturally sensitive within its limits, his vision made out the patterned spheres of an orchard on the nearest blue rise, seven miles off. Beyond and beyond the further hills, he knew ran the Delaware. His life had been spent on that river, white in morning, yellow at noon, black by supper. On the other side had stood a green rim: Pennsylvania. In those days—it would have been in the first Roosevelt's administration—when he had freshly come, direct from normal school, to teach at a building of then less than a hundred pupils, walking to work had taken him along a path from which, down the long bank through switches of sumac and sapling oak, glimpses of water had appeared as white and smooth as a plaster wall. The path ascended, passing beneath a red oak where children had attached a knotted rope and on the trunk had nailed a ladder of slats. At the highest point three shacks housing the humblest elements of the town commanded a broad view. The bank was so steep here the tops of the tallest trees clinging to it were lower than one's own shoes. The river's apparent whiteness was dissolved in its evident transparency: the contours of bars of silt and industrial waste could be easily read beneath the gliding robe of water. A submerged bottle reflected sunlight. Occasionally, among the opaque fans of corrugation spread by each strand of shore growth, the heavy oblong of a catfish could be spied drifting. The family in one of the shacks did woodcutting; the air at this place in the path where Hook usually paused always smelled of sawdust, even in winter, through the snow. And across the width of water a curtain of trees hung, united with its reflection, unmarked by a house or puff of smoke. To Hook Pennsylvania had been the westerly wilderness, and when he crossed the bridge at Trenton it surprised him to encounter houses and streetcars as advanced as those in his native state.

His eyes had a thirst for water, but no amount of study would turn the blue-green hills into a river, and even were the intervening land shaved as clear as a table top, the Delaware would be hidden from him by the curvature of the earth—eight inches to the mile, as he recalled it. His education was prominent in two places: Roman history, which he had received in the grammar school of his day, and nineteenth-century American politics, talk of which had filled his father's home.

Closer to where he stood, on this side of the rough sandstone wall the women were beginning to move about on the dark grass, picking up sticks and carrying tables; foolish women, the dew would soak their feet.

"The sky suggests rain," he said, returning to Gregg in voice while not moving.

"The f.ing bastard I have half a mind to snip every one of these rotten tags off and throw them in his birdbrain face."

These wild words were not worth answering, and an answer, no matter what, would involve him deeper with Gregg. He felt distaste for Gregg: he was like a student who, having been given the extra attention due the sheep in a hundred that has strayed, then refuses to know his place, and makes of the older man's consideration a cause for a displeasing familiarity. Yet Gregg's physical aspect, and specifically the small, stained, wrinkle-hatched, dour and dangerous face that left no impression of its eyes, inspired persistent affection, reminding Hook of Harry Petree. Against Harry Petree's memory Hook abruptly shut his mind.

He said, "Aren't the women foolish now, to be setting up for the fair with a storm at their elbows? They'll be bringing in those tables before noon. No doubt Conner put them up to it."

The sense of moisture ascending was everywhere: on the sandstone walls, some stones wet and others without clear reason dry; in the odor of the freshened grass; in the amplified sound of the grackles in the maples to the left and the chatter of the women down below; in the hazy solid movements of the women. Tens of thousands of such mornings had Hook seen.

The deepening of the sky, however, above the southeast horizon, where it should be lightest, and the proclamatory weight of the slow wind that fitfully blew, were peculiar to this day.

"A bit of ago," he stated, "the sky was savage red."

Gregg raved on, "What we ought to do is take one of these tabs every day and mail it to him, a different tab every day; the post office can't refuse our custom."

"Such talk," Hook sighed, lowering himself philosophically into the chair to the left of Gregg, his customary position. Since Gregg was sitting not on the chair labelled his own but perversely in Hook's, Hook correspondingly occupied a wrong chair. When George Lucas came around the porch, from the side beneath the maples, he unthinkingly sat beside Hook, as he always did. "Have you noticed these tags?" Hook asked his other friend.

"The damn bastard Conner," Gregg shouted across, "I have half a mind to strip every one of them off."

Lucas was a fat man, yellowish in complexion, with a brief hooked nose. Young by the standards of the place, he had been a truck farmer in the southern wedge of Diamond County. His land had been requisitioned by a soybean combine organized by the Federal Department of Conservation. With the money they paid Lucas he had begun a real estate business in the nearest town, where he was well known, and had failed. He knew land but displeased people. Hook himself, charitable and gregarious to a fault, found it hard to enjoy association with Lucas, not because of the man's bluntness, but because he seemed preoccupied still with the strings of the outer world and held himself aloof from the generality of inmates. His friendship with Hook, Hook felt, served some hidden use. As a legally declared bankrupt Lucas had come to the poorhouse less than three years past, the winter of Mendelssohn's funeral. He was forever digging in his ear with a wooden match to keep an earache alive. "No," he said, "where are the tags?" As he said this an instinct made him lift the wrist beneath which the silver rectangle glittered.

"They put these on the chairs so we won't lose our way," Hook stated with irony.

"But this ain't mine, it's Benjie's chair," Lucas was saying, having read the name imbedded in the arm.

"A child like Conner must tinker endless-ly," Hook continued, deafened by his own chain of thought. He felt his wrist being lifted and his wine-dark lips quivered with being startled as he gradually brought his eyes to bear on the man inches from him.

"This is my chair," Lucas said. "You have it."

"Well, Billy is seated in mine."

"Come on then, Gregg: get up," Lucas said.

Furious, Gregg screamed between held teeth, "That son of a bitch I'd like to stick one of these tabs down his throat and listen to the f.er scream when he tried to pass it."

Bending and bowing in a variety of friezes, the three men each moved up one chair in the long row that with the earliness of the hour was full in a bar of dull bronze sun.

"Rain," Lucas said, seated again.

"Goddam it I hope it pours buckets and washes out the whole damn business. We'll see then how high and mighty Conner thinks he is."

"And have no fair?" Lucas said. "The women love it so." His wife was also at the Home.

Settled in his own chair Hook felt more in charge. "Depend upon it," he said, "there are no workmen now as there were in my day. The carpenters of fifty years ago could drive a stout nail as long as my finger in three strokes. The joints that they would fit: pegs and wedges cut out of the end of a beam to the fineness of a hair, and not split the wood though they were right with the grain. And how they would hunt, for the prongs of the old-time carriages, to find a young birch that had been bent just that way. To use the wood of a branch was considered of a piece with driving two nails where one would hold. The cut nails, you know. Then wire became common, and all their thinking was done for them by the metal manufac-turers."

"Now it's all soybean plastics," Lucas said.

"Yes: to make a juice and pour it into a mold and watch it harden. What is there in that? Rafe Beam, my father's handy man, could split a sunflower seed with his hatchet so you couldn't tell between the two halves. He used to say to me, 'Aren't you fearful of standing so close?', then he'd touch the blade to my nose, so gay-making, and show me the end of his thumb between his fingers." He demonstrated and smiled.

"Dontcha think," Gregg called to Lucas, "we ought to do something about this putting our names on the chairs like branding f.ing cattle?"

Hook resented this appeal, across him, to the other man. Lucas, deep in his ear, showed no disposition to answer, so Hook announced, "Caution is the bet-ter part of action. No doubt it is an aspect of Conner's wish to hold us to our place. An-y motion on our part to threaten his security will make him that much more unyielding. They used to say, 'A wise dog lets the leash hang limp.' It might be more politic, now, if we breathed a word to the twin, and hear his explanation. You may be sure of this: tear yours off now and a new one will be on before noon."

"The twin," Gregg said contemptuously. "He knows less what goes on in Conner's brain than we do."

"Ah, don't be that sure," Hook said. "We old fellas, we don't know the half of what goes on."

"The twin isn't even half a man he's half a moron. What I think is we ought to go up to Conner in a body and say, 'O.K., Birdbrain Conner, treat us like humans instead of stinking animals or we'll write our grievances to the government in Washington.' The post office can't refuse our custom, we aren't sunk that low yet."

Hook smiled thinly. The sun had so risen that the shadow of the porch eave was across his eyes, while his lips and chin remained in the bronze light of the haze-softened sun. His lips appeared to speak therefore with individual life, "We must bide our time. Any size-able motion on our part will make Conner that much more in-secure. Now Rafe Beam used to recite,

> 'A wise old owl
>   Sat in an oak.
> The more he heard,
>   The less he spoke.
> The less he spoke,
>   The more he heard:
> Let's imi-tate
>   This wise old bird.' "

Lucas, grimacing, had been digging into his ear, and now, watery-eyed from the pain, studied his two companions. Then, his eyes on the sulphur end of the matchstick, he said, "If you want, I'll go up to Conner and ask what his idea was."

Hook's sole answer was to draw up to his height in his chair; his face lifted entirely into shadow. The corners of his lips were downdrawn as fine as pencil points. Lucas had no fear of Conner; it was what everyone had noticed. Hook had momentarily forgotten.

"You give him this," Gregg said, and he held up and vibrated a skinny white fist, yellow in the sun, "and tell him it came from me."

CONNER'S office was approached by four flights of narrowing stairs, troublesome for these old people. Accordingly few came to see him. He intended in time to change this; it was among the duties of the prefect, as he conceived the post, to be accessible. It had not been he but his predecessor Mendelssohn who had chosen to center the executive in the cupola. Why, Conner could guess from the look of the man in his coffin and the layout of the buildings. Though the fourth flight, the last and narrowest—tan unpainted stairs rising between green walls barely a shoulders'-breadth apart—led only to the cupola and alone led away from it, once this brief diagonal descent had been made, a man could easily thread unseen through the third floor—half of it the closed doors of the bed-ridden—to the rear stairs, and thus reach the out-of-doors, and sneak behind the pig buildings and along the edge of the west wall into the adjacent town of Andrews, where Mendelssohn was well-known as a daytime drinker. The altitude of the office assured that it would seldom be visited, except by Mendelssohn's subordinates, who understood him. Further, the view commanded from the cupola was inclusive and magnificent. From what Conner had seen in the coffin—the ponderous balding head, the traces of Jewishness in the vital nostrils and the smile the embalmers had been unable to erase from the lips like the lips of a gash long healed, the faint eyebrows, the unctuously, painfully lowered lids—Mendelssohn had in part thought of himself as God.

Conner thought of no one as God. The slats of light from the east and south windows, broken into code by the leaves and stems of the plants on the sills, spoke no language to him. He had lost all sense of omen. Rising as early as Hook, he had looked at the same sky and seen nothing but promise of a faultless day for the fair. Young for the importance of his position, devout in the service of humanity, Conner was unprepossessing: the agony, unworthy of him, he underwent in the presence of unsympathetic people was sensed by them, and they disliked him for it. The ignorant came to him and reaped more ignorance; he had no gift of conversion. The theatre of his deeds was filled with people he would never meet —the administrators, the report-readers—and beyond these black blank heads hung the white walls of the universe, the listless, permissive mother for whom Conner felt not a shred of awe, though, orthodox in the way of popular humanist orators, he claimed he did. Yet there were a few—*friends*, he supposed. Buddy was one, the twin, tapping out budgetory accounts at his porcelain table in the corner of the spacious room. Frequently Conner could feel Buddy's admiration and gratitude as a growing vegetal thing within himself, fed by his every action, especially the more casual; the joking words, the moan over a tangled business, the weary rising at the end of the day to pour, out of a wax-paper cup, a little drinking water on the roots of the decorative plants—like the Venetian blinds, a post-Mendelssohn innovation. Moving in, Conner had found the office bare, drab, dirty, un-ordered: a hole where a tramp napped.

"Conner? Hey, Conner." It was Lucas's habit to come half-way up the last flight and then shout, his voice highly acoustical in the narrow enclosure. Conner did not know how to correct him; there was no bell; he did not know how they did it in Mendelssohn's day, nor did Lucas, Lucas and his wife having entered the place a month after the new prefect.

"Yes, George. Come on up." He frowned for Buddy to see and kept his hands on the piece of paper he had been reading, a letter from an anonymous townsperson. Buddy's hands ostentatiously rapped on, not compromising his noise for their visitor. The twin's brain in boyhood had been soaked in thrillers, and to him Lucas was the Informer, indispensable yet despicable.

Indeed, that Lucas, in the midst of such general hostility, should be comparatively natural with him made Conner himself uneasy. The man perhaps thought he was winning kindness for his wife, though there was no evidence that he was; impartiality with Conner was a crucial virtue. By way of comment on his puffing, Lucas said, "A lot of stairs. You'd think you were hiding."

Conner smiled mechanically, his eyes glancing to

the letter; *help not hinder, I myself,* and *rights* leaped from between his fingers. He lacked the presence, however, to hold a silence. "Martha getting her cake made?" he asked, clipping away minor words in embarrassment at being conventionally cordial.

"She's fussing at something, I know."

"You must be glad," Conner said, "that she's on her feet again." He felt this remark instantly as fatuous; of course Lucas was glad. Yet he had meant it well, and he felt irritation at the invisible apparatus that, placed between himself and any of the inmates, so scrupulously judged the content of expressions that were meant to be carelessly amiable.

To his relief Lucas removed their talk to the plane of business. "They noticed their names on the porch chairs downstairs."

Conner's heart tripped, absurdly. He should have given up hope of pleasing them long ago; it was enough to help them. Ideally, his dedication wore blinders, but he was too weak not to glance to the side for signs of approval. The sculptor has his rock and the saint the silence of his Lord, but a man like Conner who has vowed to bring order and beauty out of human substance has no third factor; he is a slave, at first, to gratitude. In time, he knew, this tender place grows callous; he had heard the older men whose disciple he was discuss, not entirely in joking, mass murder as the ultimate kindness the enlightened could perform for the others. "From your tone," he said to Lucas, "I take it their noticing should cause me anxiety."

"Well, they're confused. They can't read your purpose."

"Who is this they?"

Lucas poked something small and wooden into his ear and made a face of pain, his clayey skin eroding in rivers suddenly.

"You needn't name them," Conner added.

"Hook and Gregg were the ones I heard talking about it."

"Hook and Gregg. Poor Gregg, of course, is one notch removed from dementia. Hook is something else. Tell me, do you think Hook is senile?"

"In the head? No."

"Then there must be a rational cause that has set him against me."

"Oh, he's not against you. He just talks on the first thing that comes into his mind."

"And I'm always in his mind. What better friend does he think he has than myself? Hook's been here fifteen years; he knows what it was like under Mendelssohn."

Lucas looked startled to be feeling the edge of an apologia that was, Conner realized, principally excited by the preposterous and insulting letter he had been reading. "He speaks real well of him," Lucas said, with an odd steadiness of his eyes. "I have no opinion; I came here after you."

"Half the county home acres were lying fallow, waste. The outbuildings were crammed with refuse and filth. The west wing was a death trap. When Hook, last autumn, ate that unwashed peach, he would have died if Mendelssohn had still been in charge."

"Doesn't anybody realize," Buddy interjected in his somewhat frantic boy's voice, "what Mr. Conner has done here? This home has one of the five highest ratings in the north-eastern sector."

"I read that on the bulletin board. It makes us all

proud." Lucas's hands went to the side of his head, and his face crumpled again. This over, he asked soberly, "But now what was the idea about the name-plates?" *Dogged*, flashed on Conner as an adequate summation of Lucas.

Conner wondered if it were wisest to be silent. Words, any words, gave a person a piece of yourself. Swiftly, reasons marshalled against this unworthy impulse:

You should not make shows of authority.

Lucas, fat and blunt and coarse-pored as he was, soiling the order of this office and the morning's routine, deserved politeness, as one of the unfortunates.

If Conner fudged, Lucas would convey the fact to the others.

The question was not, as it seemed (so strong was Conner's impression this moment of defiance and ingratitude everywhere), an impudence to which there is no answer.

There was an answer; everything Conner did he did for a reason; his actions were glass.

His motives occurred to him; he stared at the shine on Lucas's taut hooked nose and then shot his gaze to the stripes of blue at the window, saying, "There have been complaints, *a* complaint—one of the women came to me, in regard to her husband—that on rainy days the men who work on the farm can't find chairs on the porch, or at least the chairs they think of as their own. The vacant chairs are scattered, so some are unable to sit with their friends. It's childish, of course. Mendelssohn, I'm sure, would have laughed her away. But I—my duty is to take all complaints seriously.

Part of my policy has been, within the limits of the appropriations, to give the residents here some sense of ownership. I think especially of men like Hook, who have known a share of respect and prosperity. It strengthens, is my belief, rather than weakens a communal fabric to have running through it strands of private ownership. Lucas, I want to help these men to hold up their heads; to retain to the end the dignity that properly belongs to every member, big or little, of humanity."

He pivoted in his socketed chair and saw that in his typing corner Buddy was blushing jealously, to hear his superior speak with such fervor to an interloper. The boy (so touching, his blurted proclamation of their fifth-place honors) had perhaps assumed that the image of the thread of private property and the hope concerning dignity to the end had been a confidence shared between just the two of them. It would not do for Conner to explain, by even so much as the tone of his eyes, that in this instance, without disbelieving his words, he was using them more for their impact than their sense, more to keep Lucas at a distance than convey a creed. When Conner had been Buddy's age he would have been repelled by any revelation to the effect that within the outer shell of a man's idealism is fitted a shell of cynicism; within this shell, another, contracted compared to the first, of idealism, and so on down, in alternate black and white, to the indivisible center; and that it is by the color of the star here alone that the course of a man's life is set. Obliquely mitigating his unintended offense to Buddy, Conner mentioned his name in continuing to Lucas, "Mr. Lee, with a few of the other women, took much trouble in fixing each man's favorite chair. In some cases the old men themselves sat in a new place every day. The present arrangement is a work of love on his part. And yet Hook takes it as a cause of complaint. This is the reward Mr. Lee receives for the devotion he brings to his work in this institution; in private or semi-private industry his talents would earn him three times his present salary."

"Well, I'll tell them," Lucas said, though his attention for the last minute had been turned toward the inside of his head.

Perhaps still appeasing Buddy, Conner asked sharply, "What in hell are you doing to your ear?"

"A little soreness." Lucas went on the defensive; his head bowed and the pink inner skin of his cumbersome lower lip showed.

"For how long?"

"Not long."

"A day? Two?"

"I guess longer."

"You've been running an earache for longer than two days. What medication have you received?"

No answer.

Conner answered for him, "None."

"I've had a soreness, off and on, for some time."

He might have been speaking of an animal he had befriended. "Well, could you go to the west wing *now*, please? And throw the matchstick into the wastebasket. *This* wastebasket. Good God, you'll give yourself otomycosis." Conner hated, more than anything, pain dumbly endured. Oppression, superstition, misery—all sank their roots in meekness.

Lucas, turned into a child by this undeserved streak

of rebuke, left as commanded. Conner, grieving for the bad temper brought on by the uneasy conscience unjustly forced on him by Buddy's sulk and the letter on his desk, rose and stood by the east windows and looked down through parted blinds to people foreshortened on grass. On the east, south, and west sides, the cupola had big windows, sets of three with round-arched tops, the middle one taller than the two flanking. The metal supporting the Venetian blinds muddled the stately lines, and the semi-circles, each fitted of five pieces of hand-worked wood, peeked above the manufactured horizontals like the upper margin of a fresco painted where now an exit has been broken through the wall. On the fourth side, the north, the steep stairway climbed from the floor below, contained within the external silhouette of the cupola, so that the door came into the room, making on each side of it an alcove, in which a simpler window had been let. Light at all times of the day came into the room; each standing object in it became a sundial, which no one there could read. The man, Walter Andrews, who seventy years before had built the mansion had meant this for the piano room; the system of supports and joints above had been left free, diagonal rafters and slender crossbeams where music could entwine, and the musicians grouped around the piano below could play on and on, feeding the growing cloud above without having their noise press out from the walls and crowd them. The piano was still in the room, underlying terraces of green steel cabinets. There was no way of getting it out; it had been hoisted up and set on the bare floor when the room was unfinished. Where the east set of windows were the next day placed, the wall was open on blue air, the ends of the golden boards making a ragged hole in which the romantic black piano-shape appeared, a miracle, the ropes too thin it seemed, the workmen apprehensive, a breeze blowing, the points of the tapered legs tracing a fugal phrase *largo* on the emptiness as the huge instrument gently twirled in its secure cradle of rope. The piano within, the workers completed the well-knit wall, Andrews giving no consideration to the day after tomorrow or to the species that would follow his.

The tall space above, crossed with stained beams, catered to a kind of comfort not proper to executive and clerical work. Conner came from a world of low ceilings, onion-gray or egg-blue, made still lower by fluorescent structures. The space below made him uneasy, too. "Damn these people," he said, his lips an inch from the sharp blond edge of a subtly curved slat of the blinds. "Now down there's Hook, making his rounds like the mayor of the place, talking to everybody, stirring them up for some crusade."

To Buddy, watching, the profile of his superior was incisive against the luminous blinds: the little round nose above the long bulging lip of an Irishman, in saddened repose. In his rush of love Buddy had to speak, any words, and the first words came to him from what was bearing on his mind, "Don't you think we could dispense with Lucas? He learns more than he tells, and physically, you must admit, he's a monstrous error."

"AH, Mrs. Jamiesson," Hook said, "don't the apples shine in your cheeks this morning? That's what

Ed Hertzog used to say, when greeting the women after church service."

She was tacking an oilcloth frill to the front edge of the bare table she had set in the grass, and he was standing in her way. "Could you hold that there with your fingers?" she asked him.

"De-lighted, posolutely delighted," he said, mimicking someone else, a normal school chum, forty years dead, named Horace Frye. His downward vision was so poor he set his fingers along the naked edge of wood, and when Mrs. Jamiesson went with her hands for the hammer and tacks, the scalloped strip fell, the unfastened end of it into the drenched grass. As if managing a baby and his spoon she laid her tools aside and gripped his hand and brought the cloth to it and pressed his fingers against the edge. He let her drive one tack and stood away, his eyes on the top of the silver maple by the west wing. "That sound," he announced, "is music to my ears; the carpenters in my day would drive a coarse nail with three swift strokes."

"Well I guess I'm not one of them," Mrs. Jamiesson said. She was a heavy woman whom homeliness had trained to a life of patience and affection. It was a wonder to her mother that this daughter, with the freakishly protuberant jaw, had married and held the man and raised a family. The waspish temper she had inherited from her beautiful mother Mary Jamiesson had repressed, a luxury she had to do without. Yet a lively tongue never quite dies. "It's a rare sight for me," she went on, "to see a man do any work; else I guess I'd learn something."

Hook did not miss the sense of her remark, only its application to him. "It's the admini-stration," he confided. "To let a man choose idleness or labor, on the ground of whim: why in Mendelssohn's time such a thing would never be seen. Able-bodied men like Gregg and Lucas—it's a wonder they haven't grown too lazy to lift the food to their mouths at mealtimes."

"Lucas has the pigs, though." Mrs. Lucas was a companion of hers.

"What day's work is that, to carry the garbage from the kitchen to the trough?"

"Well it's more than some do," Mrs. Jamiesson observed.

Uneasiness crept over Hook. The woman's implication—that women did the work of the place—was disagreeable to him, like a scent which raises the fine hairs on an animal. "Isn't it strange now, the only muscle which never tires is the tongue," he said, and moved on, forgetting who had begun this train of remarks. The long-grass lawn, now that the sun had moved higher, turned toward yellowness; in the center of the main walk, two old men were slowly unravelling electric cords, cardboard boxes of colored bulbs behind their legs. A stepladder lay flat in the grass. One of the men fumbled at a snarl as if this were his sole task for all the time remaining in God's scheme. A robin scolded *wheep wheep* in the tree nearby. Beyond the south wall, the landscape extended itself generously; deliberate stands of trees were dotted like islands over the land; a few houses, outreaches of Andrews, intruded their colors on the left edge of his aimed vision. He coughed and stated, "Now I can remember," and noticed he was standing alone. He moved closer to the men on the walk. The one not fiddling with the snag was removing bulbs from their beds of tissue paper and laying them, so that no two of the same color touched, on the bench. "Now I can remember, as a boy, how you could go to the top of a hill and not see a house in an-y direction. Now"—he coughed again, since the heads of neither had moved—"there can't be a foot of earth east of the Alleghenies where a body can stand and not be within hailing distance of a house. We have made the land very tame." Hook cocked his head inquisitively. He decided he had picked two deaf ones. Their names escaped him.

Turning away, he felt like a rise of unplowed land which approached from below swells unexpectedly and in a spattering of daisies makes a join with the sky. All the movements of preparation around him gladdened him. He was glad of Gregg's absence; the man had gone to the kitchen, to wheedle a second breakfast. There was one lack, one shallow pit in the surface of his pleasure: he had no cigar in his hand. He allowed himself four a day, and in the discussion over the tags had neglected to light his morning one; he did this now, a White Owl. The barn odor filled his mouth; he posed, cupping the elbow of his cigar arm in his other hand, the other arm braced gracefully against his abdomen.

The wooden tables—their eating tables before the dining hall was fitted with square tables of synthetic marble purchased from a renovated cafeteria—were arranged partly along the main walk, but principally in two alleys at right angles to the walk, straight across the grass. Because the old people did it the lines were not absolutely straight. Hook strolled down one of these alleys, angling the cigar this way and that in friendly fashion. By Amelia Mortis's table he halted. She was a short old woman, in her eighties and thus not far from Hook himself, who wore an ancient stiff bonnet and had a goiter hanging around her neck. Each year she made from rags a few quilts, perhaps six in all, which she sold each August at the fair. Last year a man from Trenton had bought four.

"Do you expect your sharper from Trenton again this year?"

"I hope to heaven not. It makes it so dull to have them sold so quick."

"That fella, dollars to doughnuts he was one of those antique dealers, and peddled them for thrice what he paid you."

"Last year it was so disappointing; he bought all I had left and there was nothing left for me but to go to bed and miss all the music." Her voice had a crooning quality, as if it originated deeper than most and rose through a screen; she had a tendency to let the ends of her sentences impatiently drop, which led Hook to bend toward her.

"I wager," he said, "he made a ver-y hand-some profit."

"I like to see the young couples have them, but you know how they care only for the new things. I was the same way myself."

One of her quilts, folded, rested on the table. The remainder were in two boxes labelled with the name of a dehydrated milk. At the end of a year of threading and biting and matching, she stretched the simple arrangement of them on the table into a full morning's job, refolding, patting, replacing them in the boxes, dawdling and turning until she felt quite dizzy and had to beg for a chair. Of the quilt displayed, one square was of a cloth on which a green hill had been printed, covered with uncommonly large flowers, and a river wound at its base, and on its crest had been planted a small open temple, the blue of the sky showing between the pillars. This figure had been repeated over the fabric. The square of cloth next to this one was evenly dark, the color of purple vetch. Next to this was a coarse plaid weave, many colors but sober, the largest stripe a green, making in the section a cross. The first square of the next row, beneath the temple and hill, seemed silk, a blue that appeared to retreat beyond the surface of the cloth, dotted with warm rectangles and crescents. The next patch was savage red; violently strewn across it strange golden forms like a carved alphabet or furniture molding. Another square showed children running carrying a pail. Another was brown corduroy, another green cotton. Another—here Hook disbelieved. The violet ground, the five yellow ovals around a blue five-point star, within a brown square, again and again, were too much like his childhood bedspread for belief—the very dusty grape tone, the nameless flowers seen so squarely from above. In the confused way of recollections from that time he saw himself as a child wandering among the rectilinear paths of the pattern, searching for the deeper-dyed thread that occasionally, in the old woven cloth, would arch above the others. In the rough-walled room lit by kerosene, the wick kept thriftily low, he saw the coverlet waiting for him; it was evening, he was a child. His parents were down below; his father's voice shook softly up the stairs. He felt no great resentment, for as a serious-minded child he feared the dark but knew that he must sleep, when the time came each day. Studying the cloth Hook felt the small condensed grief—that the past was so far, the end so near—secreted safe within his system well up and fill his head so exactly the thin arcs of his eyes smarted with what they contained. He blinked rapidly, erasing the glow of that kerosene lamp.

"Now how Mendelssohn," he said, "would have stroked and patted this quilt."

"Wouldn't he though? He gave me such encouragement."

"It was his way."

"He was like McKinley," Mrs. Mortis exclaimed, invoking a girlhood idol of hers, "for dignity, yet he was never too busy to drop a kind word." Her face in the shadow of the bonnet was uplifted rhapsodically. "That's how you know them, John."

Her high tone, and his old debater's instinct, prompted him, above his fundamental agreement, to enter a qualification. "They say, you know," Hook said, "that in regards to admini-stration, he would let a few things slip. But in his day there wasn't such idleness as you see now."

"Ah, and often I can picture him in the mind's eye saying grace," she continued, her goiter bouncing like the breast of a clucking chicken, "with his eyes downcast so gracious, and his voice booming out so even the deafest could hear; in his coffin, I remember saying to Mrs. Haines, he looks like he's come to the end of a prayer, his nostrils still full of its breath. My heart told me to stoop and kiss his hand, but the line was pushing."

"He had a natural faith—"

"You know them when you come across them, rare as that is. Oh, we've had our time, John."

Hook did not think it was a woman's obligation to tell him he had had his time. Amy Mortis was a woman of his own generation—she would have been marriageable to him—and along with the corresponding virtues she had the talkativeness, the presuming habit, the *familiarity* of such women; calling him "John." He enjoyed conversing with them, but not as much as they with him, nor for as long. Yet as with his late wife, he was too weak, too needful of her audience to break away, and instead lingered to lecture.

"Now, that McKinley was nothing but Mark Hanna's parade uniform; the man he beat was twenty times his greater, and he did it on the strength of New York and Boston money. Bryan."

"Yes, one of those wanting to steal everything from the rich and give it to the poor and now that they've done it, are we better off? Are the poorhouses empty? Why, no: they're building more and still they're crowded. I feel so sorry for the younger women, having to share those tiny rooms. Young Bessie Jamiesson lying down at night with Liz Gray, who hasn't washed herself in human memory. And the Lucases and that bird keeping for themselves a room that would do for four humans."

Having forgotten what he wanted to say, Hook shook his head negatively and thoughtfully pulled on the cigar. The metallic cloud, as good as any sensible masculine argument, hung in the air between them, then snapped away. Taking his time within the won advantage, he pronounced, "Were Mark Hanna still running the country, good lady, our kind would be dead long past."

"Yes and wouldn't it be an improvement," she said with great readiness, as if she had been impatiently watching the sentence take form in his head. "We hang on and hang on and spend our time on such foolishness"—a scrabbly motion indicated the quilts—"when if we had any sense we'd let the Lord take us and start us off fresh."

"You don't antici-pate, then, any difficulties, on the other side?"

The suggestion in his tone that there was crudeness in her religion irritated her. She said, "Well, if there are for me, few'll pass," showing that in asking her rights she could be as testy with the Lord as with any other man. "I've been as good as most."

"Ah, yes," he said, breathing admonitory smoke, before the comedy of her spunk occurred to him, and his mustache broadened, and he promised her that if, as was likely, he got there before her, he would certainly save her a place on the settee. Making this guarantee he bowed with cocky gallantry above the nearly dwarfish figure of the good lady. There vibrated between them something of the attraction he had of old exercised on members of the opposite sex.

THE ENTRY DOOR to the west wing whispered shut behind Lucas and he was frozen. There was white on both sides of him, extending like the repetition of a few beds in double mirrors, with increasing dimness, to the end beds by the Palladian windows, which shed on the linen a pearly, generalized light. The west wing did not get the sun directly until the latter part of the day. The figures beneath some of the sheets made faint movements; a skeletal arm lifted to gain attention, a pink scrubbed head turned listlessly to take in the new entrant. The sheets did not seem to have beneath them persons but a few cones, from the points of which the folds sloped apparently to the mattress, and Lucas thought of parts of bodies—feet, the pelvis, shoulders without arms—joined by tubes of pliable glass, transparent so the bubbling flow of blood and yellow body juices could be studied. The impression was upon him before he could avert his eyes. Incapable of any retreat he looked on the floor, fearful above all of accidentally finding among the composed faces of these ailing and doomed the face of an acquaintance, someone with whom he had shared a talk on the sunporch, or walked into Andrews with. On the floor his helpless eyes noticed the marks made by the soft wheels of the stretcher-wagon. Even more than black death he dreaded the gaudy gate: the mask of sweet red rubber, the violet overhead lights, the rattling ride through washed corridors, the steaming, breathing, percolating apparatus, basins of pink sterilizer, the firm straps binding every limb, the sacred pure garb of the surgeons, their eyes alone showing, the cute knives and angled scissors, the beat of your own heart pounding through the bur- nished machinery, the green color of the surgeon's enormous compassionate eyes, framed, his quick breath sucking and billowing the gauze of his mask as he carved. Carved. Surgeons bent over you like lions gnawing the bowels of a deer. Lucas had watched his father die of cancer of the bowel. It was the family death, for males.

Many of the heads suspended on the white waves were turned to him by now. Lucas, with his big body and strange skin, was not inconspicuous. Dr. Angelo came up to him silently. "Yes?"

The doctor was a middle-aged Italian, highly handsome, though his head was a bit too big for his body, and his eyes for his head. It was as if the years of service and fatigue that had subdued his Latin mannerliness to mere staring, indeed dazed, gentleness had also been a drag on his lower lids: his green irises rode a boat of milk, under a white sky. Thus his eyes were targets.

"Conner thought I should come here."

"Why did Conner think that?"

"No reason, except to get me out of his way."

Angelo waited, the beautiful mouth smiling regretfully beneath the two ovals of gray hair symmetric on his upper lip. He held some cards in his hands but showed no sign of being interrupted. "Is the difficulty rectal?" he at last suggested.

"Oh, hell, no. No. It's just my ear. A little itching that comes and goes now and then."

"Could we have a look? Come over here, Mr.—?"

"Lucas. George R."

"Yes. You have a wife. Did her legs improve?"

"Wonderfully. We're both wonderful. The ear doesn't pain at all now, but I guess that's always the way."

"Mm." Angelo led the way to his office, a brown desk shielded by frosted glass partitions, but open in the front. One entire pane was papered with licenses, permits and certificates of authority from state and federal bureaus.

"This ear?"

"The other."

Angelo inserted the nozzle of a brass funnel painfully deep into Lucas's head and murmured with a trace of pride, "Definitely inflamed. How have you been irritating this canal?"

"I try to keep it clear of wax," Lucas admitted, his voice made flat, loud, and hollow by the cold metal in his ear.

"How is the other?"

"First-rate. Never a twinge or anything."

"May we see?" And the frightening operation was repeated. Lucas wanted all metal to keep away from his body. With a certain brutality the icy intruder in his head squirmed, and Angelo's wet breath beat on the side of his neck. "Nothing," Angelo decided finally.

Lucas was sufficiently relieved to observe across the aisle from the office a gaunt woman, of seemingly prodigious length, switching her head back and forth on the pillow, as regular as a pendulum.

"Let's try this," Angelo said. A soft rubber mask was clapped over the bad ear; he winced. "Tender?" Angelo asked.

"A little, but you know . . . nothing." It occurred to him, with a muffled inner jolt, that his ear was quite badly off; would have to be lanced. He had heard rumors all his life of this operation; nothing was more painful. It was brief, they said, a mere moment, an atom of pain, but of such pain as couldn't be bettered; the prick pierced all the layers of numbness right through to the ultimate, blue-hot sheet of pain that set the limit to suffering.

Angelo threw a switch at the side of his desk, by the radiator. "Just tell me the numbers you hear."

Lucas figured that if he passed this test he would be let off the lancing. At first it was easy. The voice was a woman's, very slow and ticky, like a phone operator's. He repeated after her, "13 . . . 74 . . . 5 . . ." Her voice grew higher as she sank into a lake of viscid substance. "12," she called, "99." In the strain of listening the rustle of blood in his head created static. "Uh, 99." His tongue had become queerly cumbersome; his heart fluttered high in his chest. He missed the woman's next two cries, so deep and tiny had she grown. The head across the aisle turned left, then right on the pillow, like a wingbeat. Lucas ventured, "80?"

Angelo impatiently tore away the rubber cup. In his anxiety Lucas had pressed it hard against his skull; his ear smarted.

"Grace," Angelo called. "Grace!" To the girl who appeared he said, "Lucas. George R., please."

His eyes settled into fixity. The two irises enlarged and merged into one great opaque black pupil circled by considerate green, which shield pressed against Lucas's chest. Wriggling under this weight of attention Lucas's mind desperately sought to gain a glimpse of the phantom Grace and whatever cruel instruments she was bringing. How could he know what grim message the simple syllables of his name, in Angelo's mouth, had spelled to her? Smiling tirelessly, Angelo explained in monotonously intoned detail the clinical nature of his aural morbidity. Lucas caught none of it, except when Angelo, in specifying the location of the worst redness, made a circle with his thumb and forefinger and with a finger of the other hand rubbed the wrinkly part of the thumb skin and said, "Right in around here. Between seven and eight o'clock." A queer trick, his making the ear a timepiece; there was something insane in so much explanation.

All Grace brought was a blue card. Making swift marks on it, Angelo asked if he had ever had that upper molar pulled. Two years ago it had been noted as dead and liable to abscess.

"It never gave me no trouble."

"A submerged infection doesn't always declare itself to the nervous system. There are instances of an abscess at the root of a tooth—up in here, you see—" he touched one half of his mustache—"inserting poison into the bloodstream until the host suffers a coronary. Will you make an appointment please with Dr. Duff's secretary, you know the office? The second door to the left as you leave the ward." While saying this he fussed in his desk. "Now. Steady, please."

He came at the side of his eye with something long and thin.

Lucas reared away, half-rising.

Angelo smiled. The heavy beauty of his face loomed beyond a small rod of cotton-tipped wood, which he held up for Lucas to see. "We're going to apply a little zinc to ease the irritation." He did this, inserting the warm gray unguent with a careful twirling motion that tickled intimate turnings dangerously near, Lucas felt, seats of pain. But Angelo, godlike, resisted the temptation, so understandable to Lucas at this moment, to prod a sensitive spot. He was soon done. He gave Lucas a small silver tube, several wooden wands, and a wad of cotton wrapped in orange tissue. The ointment was to be applied three times a day. If the trouble did not vanish in four days, return. Rolled on inertly by the sound of his voice, Angelo asked if Lucas were ready for the fair today, and said something implying that Lucas and his kind seized this annual opportunity to import hard liquor and get "a load on" behind the north wall.

Lucas had never heard of such a practice. "What year did this happen?"

Angelo looked surprised. "Every year. Don't you know about it? I forget, you're a married man."

"Oh—" Lucas felt himself expected to smirk. "I know enough. Being married doesn't mean you never lift your arm."

Angelo, for a moment uncertain, like a joking priest who has perhaps misjudged his company, laughed aloud in relief. "A patient some years ago told me that was the custom. He wanted to know if it wasn't a good idea medically. I told him it was a good idea *cos*metically. That poor fellow's gone now. In fact his insides had been gone when he came here. I was afraid for a minute the rest of you had profited by his bad example."

"Well, no," Lucas easily lied, "we try to keep up the old traditions."

Angelo liked this, and they might have gone on and on, for the thought of corruption put a sinister bloom on the doctor's manner, but luckily for Lucas there was a distraction. The woman flapping her head across the aisle called "Miss. Miss." Angelo's ponderous eyes wavered, and heavily he pushed away from the desk.

Lucas left the three-sided box—box no doubt for some the entry to smaller boxes, more intricate chairs, and the final straps beneath the violet bulbs—light-headed. Passing Grace, the nurse, he saw she was a beautiful girl of twenty or so, her body firm as a half-green apple. He seemed to skate through the white cones of the doomed, and felt himself, mirrored in the waterless eyes watching, a cruelly vital toad. He was so rejuvenated he played hooky, ignoring Dr. Duff's door and making no appointment.

HIS WORDS with Amy, and the patch of frail grape cloth, reminiscent, in her quilt, had affected Hook poorly. Her speaking so plainly of death stirred the uglier humors in him. In the mid-mornings of days he usually felt that he would persist, on this earth, forever; that all the countless others, his daughter and son among them, who had vanished, had done so out of carelessness; that if like him they had taken each day of life as the day impossible to die on, and treated it carefully, they too would have lived without end and have grown to have behind them an endless past, like a full bolt of cloth unravelled in the sun and faded there, under the brilliance of unrelenting faith. Amy, with her sharp short view, had disrupted the customary tide of his toward-noon serenity. He consoled himself by contemplating the southeast horizon, where, in support of his prediction, luminous leaning cumulus clouds were constructing themselves.

Not that the sun was diminished yet. On the meadow beyond the wall, low where Hook stood, a rabbit paused, a silhouette of two humps, without color. When the creature lifted his head his chest showed its sharp bulge, and a lilac redness was vivid within the contour of his translucent ear—as Hook saw him he had but one ear.

In the wide darkness surrounding the constricted area Hook's eyes could focus on, stars began to dance. They shut off and on with electronic rapidity, midges of dazzlement, and when he sought to give them chase, they removed their field to a further fringe of the sky his eyes made, and with a disconcerting sensation of insubstantiality he realized he had been concentrating into the sun, and that he had had little sleep the night before. He retired early but slept little, waking at queer hours with the feeling of no time having elapsed. Hook shielded his spectacles with the cigar hand and moved the three steps to the wall. Once he had a hand placed on the abrasive tepid surface of a sandstone, he lowered his lids.

The wall, its height slightly waving, like a box hedge, enclosed four and a fourth acres. On the north the rear of the stone barn served as a section of the wall, near a wide gap once for wagons, marked by two pillars, in the mortar of which the hinges of the double metal gates of the old estate were still fixed. There was a less wide entry, more for men than vehicles, also gateless now, at the front—the east—leading into the central gravel walk. On the northeast corner, nearest Andrews, a small gate was kept padlocked, though in the estate's days it had seldom been; Mr. Andrews had intended the wall and the look of the buildings to say "Mine" more than "Keep Away." The Diamond County Home For the Aged lorded over a considerable agricultural plain in New Jersey. The main building, the home, was inexactly an embroidered cube, with a shallow, somewhat hovering roof, topped by the airy cupola. The west wing, once a ballroom, looked added-on but in fact was a portion of the architect's and the second Mrs. Andrews' conceptions. The substance of the great high house was wood painted a tempered yellow weathering toward orange. To the credit of the old carpenters their work still appeared solid, without being thickly made. Along the eaves fancy trim hung, lace wheedled from pine planking. Five lightning rods were braced by spirals of hand-forged iron. The sixth had partially collapsed and pointed diagonally. Maple, horsechestnut, cherry, walnut, apple, and oak trees had grown old on the grounds. There were several broad elm stumps as memorial to the blight.

Hook prayed, requesting that the spell be allowed to pass and that his children be restored to him in Heaven. The face of his daughter occurred to him, when she was twenty-two and not married a year. He asked that he be guided to act rightly on this day. Warm color touched his lids. His mind seemed a point within an infinitely thick blanket.

Steadied, he dared open his eyes. The grass had peculiarly darkened, growing waxier, in anticipation of the rain. The cigar had died beneath the conical ash. A sense of being menaced made him look up. Gregg approached rapidly, limping as he sometimes did though his legs were sound, out of sarcastic anger or excess of energy.

"Where the hell did Lucas get to?" he asked. "Conner must have made the bastard Garbage Supervisor and we'll be lucky if he ever tips his f.ing hat to us."

Hook was pleased to have an answer. "Well: ask Conner. There he stands."

Gregg, nearsighted in the way of small people, had difficulty making out the plump figure of their prefect, where he stood at a distance, by the porch steps.

THE REVERBERATION of descending all those stairs still sounded in Conner's legs, making them feel disproportionately big. From the window, he had watched Hook perform his rounds among the old people, tried to return to work, been wounded again by the complaining contents of the letter, and let the humid importunate atmosphere Buddy was giving off get on his nerves. The air on his desk cooled; the slats of sunshine dimmed and disappeared. Returning to the window, he observed, through the blinds, a few flimsy clouds, perfectly white, strung like wash on the vapor trail of an airplane too high to see or hear. So near the ionosphere, so far from his fellow-modern watching below, was the aviator that relative to that breadth of blue his progress was imperceptible; yet the length of his trail, intact through half the firmament, bore witness to the titanic speed he was making, alone, in that airless cold.

A few clouds dropping their shadows shouldn't matter. Certainly the immense bowl above could not be filled. But Conner pictured the fair occurring in unblemished weather, like the weather on a woodcut. The weather of this one day would be, he felt, a judgment on his work; these people, having yielded all authority, looked beyond themselves for everything—sufficient food, adequate shelter, and fair weather on their one day of profit and celebration. He would be blamed, and strangely felt prepared to accept the blame, for foul skies.

He should be with them, his people. By default Hook was capturing the domain. Conner's jealousy deepened. And the aura of holiday, the general dislocation of duties, infected him, and he began the flights of stairs, but not so suddenly Buddy did not communicate, through the simple pink oval of his face caught in the corner of Conner's eye as he seized the doorknob, amazement.

Once out in the open he wondered how he could help, then realized it was not in his position to help. The emotion that had led him down had been proprietorial and aristocratic; one of the ancient men he included had spoken a word and he had followed and been abandoned on the steps, in the sunshine. He was in command only figuratively. In the long era of Mendelssohn's indifference the old people had worked out the business of the fair so they needed little interference. On the third Wednesday of August, such and such was done, regardless of who reigned in the cupola.

Conner stood by two men screwing, with painful slowness, colored bulbs into sockets strung on long cords. They were maneuvering this chore in the dead center of the main walk. Surely they needed at least advice or one of the nimbler men—Gregg, for instance, who had been, come to think of it, an electrician in Newark—to mount the shaky ladder lying on the lawn, stained by dew, when the time came to string the lights on the posts. He asked aloud how they proposed to get them up. The two went on fumbling without replying.

Conner proceeded down the walk, to where the tables began across the grass. He observed that the tables were poorly aligned, and suggested that a few be shifted slightly. Neither fastidious nor silly, he himself helped, physically, move the tables. He wondered what kind of impression this made and did not see how it could be other than good. His intentions were wholly good. Refreshed, he stood a moment by the stand of Tommy Franklin, who filed peachstones into small baskets and simple animals. Tommy himself was away; his handiwork littered the table casually, strewn on the silver boards like brown pebbles taken from a creek-bottom by the handful.

He was conscious of Hook and Gregg at the end of the alley, conferring by the wall. Under their gaze he turned to Mrs. Mortis; she was sitting in a chair and looked unsteady with her absurd towering bonnet. He asked her how she was feeling.

"No better than an old woman should."

"An old woman should feel fine," he offered, smiling: she seemed more accessible than many of the others. "Especially one who can display these lovely quilts."

"They aren't the best I've done; it's hard to get figured rags; so much of this new cloth is plain. It's all made for the young, you know; they want the simple dresses to show off their figures."

Some of the patches she had used seemed so fragile and dry he feared the sun beating from above might shred them. She herself seemed that way; the wire hoop giving her bonnet shape was wearing through; the exterior had faded while on the inner side the pattern was preserved clearly. "Wouldn't you prefer a table underneath the trees? You're in a rather exposed position here."

"Well, if I weren't exposed who'd see me?"

"I meant simply up by the walk, in the shade."

"I'm usually situated here."

"If you prefer it . . . though of course there's no difference. I only thought you looked a little pale."

"What do you expect at my age? You expect too much from us old people, Mr. Conner."

His cheek smarted, but he had never found the reply to blunt injustice. "I do?"

"You expect us to give up the old ways, and make this place a little copy of the world outside, the way it's going. I don't say you don't mean well, but it won't do. We're too old and too mean; we're too tired. Now if you say to me, you must move your belongings over beneath the tree, I'll do it, because I have no delusions as to whose mercy we're dependent on." The goiter, from which he had kept his eyes averted, swayed disturbingly: inert but still living flesh.

"That's just the way I want no one to feel. I'm an agent of the National Internal Welfare Department and own nothing here. If it is anyone's property it is yours. Yours and the American people's."

"The American people, who are they? You talk like Bryan; Hookie's always talking him up to me."

"There is no reason," Conner said, with a sensation of repetition that made him stammer, "unless you want to, why you should stand under the sun for ten hours."

"This isn't an all-day sun."

"Whether it is or not, let me and one of the men move your table and chair underneath the trees." A shadow with the cooling quality of treeshade fell over them. He looked up while she studied him; the cloud obscuring the sun had a leaden center. In great vague arcs a haze was forming in the sky. Near the eclipsed sun a cirrus cloud like a twisted handkerchief was dyed chartreuse; the phenomenon seemed little less eerie for being explicable, as iridescence.

"The chair's not mine; I borrowed it for a second, until the giddiness passed."

He pressed, "It will take just a minute."

She smiled absently, then said, girlishly direct and flirting her head, "If you think up there in the shade I'll take off my bonnet because I make this place look like a fool, I won't because when they come from in town they expect to find fools out here. Anyway I'm half bald."

Vividly, comically conscious of his own thick hair, from the black roots of which the heat of a blush poured down over his face, Conner said, "You're nothing like a fool." In these words he committed his worst error with her. He felt in the air between them her patience with him snap. Previously she had been trying him, tentatively, testing him against her memory of Mendelssohn. The game lost, he spoke more in his own voice. Haughtiness showed. "You have free will. I'm not trying to steal your bonnet from you, or your usual place; I had only your welfare in mind. But we'll let things as they are."

He continued down the alley of tables, obscurely obliged to speak to Hook. It was Hook, after all, who had compelled him to venture down into this unsafe area hours before he was needed. Self-denying by doctrine, he walked against the slope of his desire, which was for retreat into the buildings and up the narrow solacing stairs to his office.

Yet the spot where Hook and Gregg had been standing was vacant, or seemed so until with a shock he saw the cat. A caramel tom, it held one useless foreleg crooked before its chest, and its face was mashed and infected. An eye was either gone or swollen shut. Three brown snaggle-teeth hung slant-wise beneath a rigidly lifted lip.

It looked like the work of an automobile. Another cat could not have produced that crushed effect. The modern cars, run by almost pure automation, became accustomed to the superhighways and sped even on decayed lanes like the one curving past the poor-house. Conner wondered that the animal had lived. To judge from the advance of the infection the accident had occurred days ago. A disease seemed mingled with the wounds.

It was uncanny, considering the smallness and in-humanity of the face, that there should be distinctly conveyed to Conner, through the hair and wounds, an impression of a request, polite, for mercy.

Though he didn't move, the cat abruptly danced past him, bobbing like a cheap toy, keeping to the long grass near the wall. Conner wondered how he had gotten within the wall.

HOOK'S BLOOD felt thick and dark with this hurrying and confusion. His eyesight seemed further impaired; he saw nothing, in the sense of focus, but received an impression of green as his eyes by habit searched the ground before his feet for obstacles. Gregg beside him was a malevolent busy force in whose power he had unaccountably been placed. Hook felt incapable of leaving the smaller man's orbit. It was better to remain with Gregg than to stay behind and risk association with the cat. Gregg had seen it wandering in the field beyond the wall and like a boy of twelve had scrambled over the wall and captured it. Hook wouldn't have thought he could have captured it, but the creature offered no resistance, merely limped a few yards and then waited. Gregg cradled it in his arms and dropped it over the wall, near Hook's feet; Hook saw that the animal was hopelessly out of order. What did Gregg want it for? To torment, no doubt. He recalled how some of his students, in the days of the smaller school, had beaten a flying squirrel with hockey sticks during recess. Breaking up the screaming ring he had found at its center a grey pelt wildly pulsing with the parasitic life that refused to loosen its grip, and had had to dispatch it himself, weeping and trembling, with a hatchet brought up from the basement, while the pupils were within with their books. As he imagined it there had been a storm brooding that day; children invariably became unruly under the approach of wet weather.

They were hurrying because Gregg, on fire with his idea, was going to the kitchen to beg scraps for his new pet. Hook, bewildered by the sudden introduction of the animal into his morning study, had gone with him a distance, but at the corner of the big house, he realized it would not do to accompany him further. "You proceed," he said, "I want nothing to do with such monkey business."

"Okay, Hookie," the little man said, rudely using a nickname Hook had overheard before but always chose to forget, "You stay here and keep an eye on the tiger. Don't let the cops see it before I give the word."

Fanciful talk. Gregg imagining that a lame cat on these acres would be observed. Superimposing his memory of difficult students on Gregg, he perceived the true motive for his act: it was a disturbance of accustomed order. In abruptly vaulting the wall and dropping at Hook's feet this live responsibility he was making a sardonic comment on the elder man's brittle ways, which could not comfortably deviate a hair from worn paths. Hook smiled to himself. It was different now; teaching school, he had been bound to the students, but here there was no law forcing him and Gregg into association. It did not occur to him that, though Gregg in part may have been teasing his stately old friend, it was Conner's authority the cat's presence flaunted.

Obediently—in a life as empty of material purpose as Hook's, there was little substance to resist any command—he fixed his gaze on the spot far down the wall, where they had been standing. Though his sight possibly deceived him, there was no cat there. He was principally pleased. At his age it was not difficult to believe he had imagined the entire incident, and the cat in his misery was phantasmal. To strengthen his case against Gregg's certain reproval, he scanned all the distant terrain this side of the wall, looking especially under the tables and around the feet of the women. Nothing but trod lawn. The sky in the southeastern quarter was unmistakably darkening now; the thunderheads had moved up into the sky, grounded no longer on the horizon but jutting from the dense atmosphere like blooms trailing their roots in murky water.

In fact at the moment he first looked the cat was within yards of his feet, and while he inspected the distance the cat had passed his ankles and gone and hidden among the sheds in the back of the house. Hook, blind in all directions but the forward one, was vulnerable to approach from below. He was amazed when a voice by his side spoke.

"Good morning, Mr. Hook."

"Eh? Ah, Mr. Conner; pardon my not responding. I would make a better lamp-post than a spy."

"Are you admiring the view?" Conner was a head shorter than he, with a smooth face that had little harm in it, discounting the sureness and appetite of the young. His eyes were a remarkably light brown.

"Why, yes. It seems overcast."

"I'm hoping that the clouds will be blown around to the west."

A corner of Hook's mouth dimpled at the folly of

such hope. The rain was upon them now, in his mind. "The rain would be a great dis-service to the preparations," he admitted.

"WNAM predicted fair and cooler at six this morning."

"These forecasters, now,"—Hook waggled a surprisingly shapely finger upwards—"they can't quite pull a science out of the air."

Conner laughed, encouraged to be striking sparks of life from this gray monument, which had held so abnormally still as he had approached it. Then he insisted, a bit priggishly, "Everything, potentially, is a science, is it not? But it takes many years."

"More years than I likely can wait."

Conner good-naturedly held his peace. It seemed a draw. Over by an open window of the west wing a nurse laughed. The tops of the walnut trees were beginning to switch. Hook coughed. "In my boyhood, now, the almanacs would predict the entire weather for the year, day by day. Now they think it bold to to venture to say what will come within the next hour. The reports in the paper seem concerned more and more with *yesterday's* weather."

"Perhaps the weather is more variable than it used to be."

"Yes well: the bombs."

Conner nodded quiescently. He was sleepy; he rose at six, after perhaps five hours sleep—he never knew precisely, the near boundary of insomnia was vague. He hated beds; they were damp and possessive, and when he lay down, words, divorced from their objects, floated back and forth, like phosphorescent invertebrates swaying in the wash of the sea.

Day came as a reprieve. This had begun recently with Conner, in the last few years. In his sleepless state, then, he was susceptible to the contagion of his companion's pacific mood.

The figures on the front lawn, at some distance, moved in soothing patterns, silently bumping and pausing. Legs made x's when two passed each other. The activity was as ill-planned as that of an ant colony, but for the moment it did not exasperate Conner to watch. In the frame of mind of an old man idling beneath a tree, he was grateful for slow spectacles. Hook relit his cigar, now short. His eyes crossed in a look of savagery behind their magnifying lenses, and the gasps of his sucking lips assumed, in the enveloping hush, high importance. Moisture walked out from his mouth along the skin of the cigar; the nipple burned; smoke writhed across Hook's face and was borne upward.

Standing so close, and, due to Hook's eyesight, unobserved, Conner could examine the old man's face as intimately as a masterpiece in a museum: the handsome straight nose; the long narrow nostrils suggesting dignity more than vigor; the dark, disapproving, somewhat womanish gash of the mouth; and the antique skin mottled tan and white and touched with rose at the crests of the cheeks, stretched loosely over bones worn by age to a feminine delicacy. It was not the same person—compact, jaunty, busy, menacing—Conner had watched from afar, from above.

"Mr. Hook, have you seen a cat on the grounds?"

Hook's head moved not at all. In time he pronounced, "A cat with the one eye missing."

"Missing or shut. That's the one. It looked as though a car had struck him."

"Ah, isn't it a judgment, though, the way these highways are extermi-nating the wildlife? By the time you are as old as I am—not that I would wish such a fate on any-body—the sight of a rabbit or squirrel will be as rare a treat as the glimpse of a pas-senger pigeon in my boyhood."

"How did the cat get within the wall?" Hook gave no evidence of hearing. "By rights, it shouldn't be alive at all. Pathetic-looking thing."

"They cling to life extra-ordinarily. My father had a female, Becky, whose hind legs were removed by the mower, yet she lingered another six months and furthermore bore a litter of kittens. But indeed I don't believe her suffering was worth it."

"That's my feeling."

Gregg, unnoticed, had come back from the kitchen with meat scraps wrapped in orange paper. Quick to see Conner, he hid the parcel behind a post of the porch and joined them, overhearing that they were talking of the cat. He had to brave it: "What's this about my cat?"

"Why yours?" Conner asked.

Then Hook hadn't told who had brought it within the wall.

Hook said serenely, "The animal has made a get-away."

"Have you seen it, Mr. Conner?" Gregg asked politely, and continued, less politely, "I guess the damn thing was coming to the fair."

"Yes, I saw it by the wall, and it ran past me.

Someone, I think, should put it out of its misery."

"Or else put a tag around its neck," said Gregg, alluding too subtly to the nameplates on the porch chairs.

"What?" Conner had difficulty understanding the excited enunciation of this man.

"Probably it'll be the only goddam thing to come to the fair today, with the storm," Gregg went on, nearly crazy with his own boldness in the face of the fact of Conner's being right there. "If I could catch it," he cried, "I'd wring its f.ing neck."

"If a group of children were to find the animal," Hook spoke out of his memories, "they would make uncommon sport of him."

The idea sickened Conner, children soaking the dying animal with kerosene. He lacked most men's tolerance for cruelty, their ability to blur and forget rumors of it. He wondered if Gregg were ugly enough to make good his insane threat. Perhaps he was; a net of dark wrinkles had been thrown across his face, and his features seemed bright things caught in this net. Conner asked him, "Why would you harm the animal?"

Gregg was taken aback. In tides as variable as those of astrological influence, sense and caution flowed in and out of him; comparatively lucid, he realized he was facing the tyrant of the place and had been saying whatever came first to his tongue. Now Conner had taken him up, ready with a trap. "Why because," he answered, inspired, "it spreads disease."

Conner blinked; this was true.

"Among chickens," Hook interceded, "I've seen the fever brought into the pen by a fox spread so there weren't a half dozen standing by morning."

"Yes, and to humans too," Gregg went on, cleverly sensing he had found a sore spot of Conner's. "Don't they carry typhoid? If Alice sees it, sure as s. she'll let the stinking thing play around in the kitchen." His eyes glinted, and he did a dance step, unable to keep his feet from jubilating.

The cat had not gone far, once it felt unpursued. While the men talked, it returned, having smelled the parcel Gregg had laid behind the porch pillar. Alice had not tied the parcel, so it had unfolded of itself. The scraps—pork, minced—smelled neutrally to the cat; he recognized them as life-stuff, unconnected with pleasure. Dutifully he nosed the chunks, searching for lean; his bowed grave head half-lost in the collar of upstanding orange paper.

"Look there," Gregg cried softly.

As the three men watched, the tomcat, jiggling his head, got the smallest piece between his teeth, on the side where they were not smashed. But the arc his jaw could make was too small for chewing, and the piece dropped back among the others. The thin yellow tail swished twice. For a moment he licked a hump of gray fat, then lost interest wholly, looked up, saw the men, bolted off the porch, and hobbled around the house into the shade.

"Who put the meat there?" Conner asked.

"I brought a little up from the kitchen," Gregg admitted, thinking that now he was in for it.

Conner realized how badly he had misjudged the man; the culpability of the distrust he bore these powerless old people, whom complete material deprivation had not deprived of the capacity for such acts of kindness, was borne upon him. He wished there were some feasible way of abasing himself before Gregg, and he tried to compress all the affection and humility he felt into the gentle-spoken, "In vain, though, I'm afraid."

Relieved to hear in the tone that he would not be punished for trespassing into the kitchen, Gregg did not comprehend the point of Conner's words.

BUDDY, feeling jilted—especially so when, less than an hour after Conner left, sunlight drained it seemed forever from the windows of the cupola—became unable to bear his solitude, and started downstairs, in Conner's cold tracks. The twin had an unspoken terror of being alone, terror so keen that, abandoned, he unwillingly animated dead things—the green steel cabinets, the buried piano, the upright objects on Conner's desk top. These summoned presences intimidated him; he expected at every moment the window to smack its lips and the water cooler to gurgle uproariously. The stairs themselves had a dreadful capacity of closing, the walls meeting the instant before he gained the broad landing. The bannister uprights and their shadows rapidly crisscrossed in a secret conversation that grew shriller as the speed of his descent increased. He broke into the open air of the porch flushed, under the eyes of several inmates, with the pink blank beauty of a Greek sculptor's boy.

Happily Conner was looking for *him*. His superior was walking down the porch, beside the receding bright-tagged chairs. "Buddy. Good. Are you busy?"

"I came down . . . the soft drink truck might arrive. He came last year before noon."

"There's a diseased cat on the grounds. The thing's in pain and should be killed."

"You're sure?"

"That's a curious question; I'm fairly sure of what I see, yes." He glanced up nervously at the blackened half of the sky. "I'm going back up until noon."

To Buddy it seemed that today Conner was always escaping him. It was the fair's fault; the decrepits had everything their way today. He protested aloud, "What do these people want a holiday for, every day is a holiday for them?"

Conner didn't answer him, except by describing where last he had seen the animal, and the direction in which it had run.

BLOND and teenage, Ted, the driver of the soft drink truck, hummed a Spanish tune in duet with the radio:

> "Eres niño y has amor,
> qué farás cuando mayor?"

It was mostly what you got on the radio now. Ted even got a little tired of all this Latin stuff. Every other movie star was a Cuban or mestizo or something, as if you had to be brown to look like anything. Some guys he knew wore "torero" pigtails standing up from the back of their heads and sprayed their hair with perfumed shellac. Ted'd be damned if he'd do this. They could call him a Puritan all they wanted.

Turning into the curved road, the asphalt of the edges crumbling into grass, Ted had a creepy sensation of heading into death's realm. The county itself was out in nowhere—farm stuff. A poorhouse in the middle of it was twice as bad. From a Spanish movie he had seen he remembered a scene showing skeletons trying to get a young man and turn him into one of them. Ted wanted to get out of this territory fast. He had another delivery before lunch, twenty miles away, not far from his home and near a luncheonette where the girls from high school, including his, gathered to eat pizza and BarBQs. He had fixed his delivery schedule so he could be there when she was; having juggled the list made him nervous. He wasn't sure there was time enough if this took long. He wasn't even sure he could find the damn place. In the movie the idea was that after you die you're not really dead until a year or so and a scientist right before he died took a drug so he would be able to walk around. Then this colony of dead people he founded had to get the body of a young man or woman every eleven days and until they needed to eat them kept them in a cave. This young guy and girl were in there together and they fell in love. These two lying chained in the cave brought Ted to thinking of his girl, Rita, and of Rita's belly, which she had shown him the night before last. She belonged to some girls' secret club in Newark called the Nuns where they took vows not to let men touch them. But if they wanted they could let men *see* sections. She had often undone her blouse before, but the night before last was the first time she had lifted her skirt and slid her silver pants down and lay there on the back seat of the car while he kneeled beside her, his hands folded in obedience at his chest. Her eyes and mouth, three shadows in a ghostly face, looked up at him kind of sadly while below, even paler and more luminous, the great naked oval between her waist and the middle of her thighs held in its center one black shadow. Remembering seeing it, the true thing, chased away all the skeletons of that lousy movie.

Finding the place turned out to be easy. He drove under some trees and the land opened up and there it was on the left: a hell of a big yellow house back from a wall. Old people were crawling around like bugs on the lawn. To give them something to talk about he speeded, squeezing the brakes on just at the entrance, so all the cases piled high behind him clattered in gallant style. The radio sang

> "Será tan vivo su fuego,
> que con importuno ruego,
> por salvar el mundo ciego—"

He switched off the ignition and with it the radio. "Hey. Amigos. Where does this stuff go?" He caught a look at himself in the side mirror. A brownpaper cigarillo hung from his lips and his crushed cap was tilted steeply over his forehead. When he set his forearm on the sill his bracelet scratched on the steel.

"Where's Buddy?" one of the women asked nobody in particular. She had a thing growing around her neck as big as a bag of groceries: God. Ted hadn't known there was a garbage dump like this left in all of New Jersey. He even felt sorry for them, living to be so old. He hoped somebody shot him when he got to be thirty.

"Some-one re-sponsible had better fetch him," a tall gent said, not moving himself.

"Aah," a small crusty-looking one said, "what's the f.ing use? Buddy doesn't know his head from his a.h.

Why do they order this p. anyway? Who in hell drinks it?" This one had a tongue in his head at least.

"Other years it goes under the trees," a woman said.

Ted asked, "What trees, señora?"

The dirty-faced man broke in furiously, "The trees down there in the meadow, forty miles away. What the hell do you think, what trees? The trees there; Jesus what the hell is your company hiring dumb kids for?"

Ted's heart raced angrily. Though his girl and the distance he had to go to her pressed on his brain, he took his sweet time inhaling sour smoke and stared the dirt-face down. He saw himself at this moment as an elegant snake. "Si," he said at last, as if in the silence he had wrung a confession from his prey. His smile, he felt, was beautiful in its serenity. "And how do I get up there, old man? Fly?"

"Fly if you can; you look the type. If they can't hire anybody except little pansies why doesn't Pepsi-Cola give up? Want me to back it up for you? Fly! —did you hear him?" The other old people made no motion to control this nut; they acted like he was their spokesman.

Ted swung down from the cab. "Look dad," he said, "you're very good, but I don't have all day. A woman's waiting for me in Newark."

"You're from Newark? I know Newark. You ever live near Canby Street?"

"No," Ted said, and blushed lightly; the quick fawning overture had made him feel, in front of these people, big and vulnerable to ridicule and slow. ·

"Did you ever get a drink in a place called the Ten

Spot, on Polk Street where the old trolley tracks used to curve? Lenny Caragannis used to run it."

"I don't remember. . . ."

"Before your time? Or are you lily-pure?"

To Ted it seemed that with this sudden searching turn the man had penetrated through his presence backwards into the chambers of his life, and the few treasures there—his mother's profile, the tolerant face of the brick wall across the alleyway from his bedroom window, Rita's skin glowing white around the cushion of tense hair—were exposed in their poverty.

Dirt-face drew very close. "Whyncha take me back with you? You're a tough kid. You're no company man, are you? You're not in love with the company. Let's go back together. Listen. This is a hellhole of a dump. You know what they do? They put tags around your ears like pigs. Hook, the kid's going to take me back."

"He'll be sorely repri-manded if it is discovered," the tall one said.

"Come on," Ted pleaded, blushing more deeply, "how do I get this junk in?" He was addressing the others over Dirt-face's head.

"Back it up through the gate," the nut insisted, dancing and brushing against Ted's shirt, "right into the porch, and then we'll be off. You and me, kid. Bang. Bang."

"Is it wide enough?" Ted asked the tall man, who looked as though he had some authority.

"Last year they backed it through," a woman said. More old women and men were slowly gathering from everywhere.

"Now don't start to cry," the small man with the

dirty-looking face said. "Why the f. does your company hire kids that can't drive even a kiddy-car? Can you only drive forward? Ram it into reverse."

Ted stepped away from him, plucked the tan butt from his mouth, let it drop at his feet, ground it into the gravel, and said effectively, "O.K."

"Slam her through, dump the p., and I'll get in the seat beside you and crouch down. Then step on it. Don't look back. Do you have a gun, kid?"

THE ONLY GUN within a mile was in fact in Buddy's hands. A .22 purchased by a gardener many years before, when foxes and groundhogs could still be seen in the countryside, the gun was kept, with a few cartridges, on a shelf of a locked closet on the second floor.

The wand of the barrel drifted pleasantly at Buddy's side as he passed between buildings and trees the many colors of which were all, under the stress of the lowering clouds, tending toward the tint of the metal. The color of the barrel seemed the base color of all things. With the lethal weapon balanced on the hooked fingers of one hand Buddy became the center of the universe. In Conner's entrusting him with this task he saw proof of the man's affection, not dreaming how much Conner would have hated to do it himself.

He stalked beneath the windows of the west wing, tall windows designed for a ballroom. He scanned stumps, overturned boxes, corded wood, and half-collapsed sheds leaning sideways, with rhomboidal doors. The thrillers he used to read for recreation began to infest his head. His stealth became exaggerated. At a corner—there was something dramatic and treacherous about a wall changing direction—he paused, fingering the bolt and testing the clip, that it was secure. The springs of the mechanism had grown stiff with rust. The clip probably wouldn't feed the next bullet into the bolt, if he missed with one shot. Buddy stepped around the corner, and there was the cat, not twenty feet away, in the center of an open area strewn with chopping chips. It astonished him how close things looked in this foreboding atmosphere. The cat's face—he could see every whisker and wet streak on it—loomed like a china plate in a shooting gallery.

Holding one leg off the earth, the cat, while staring at Buddy, didn't act as if it noticed him. Just as Buddy had the broad forehead steadied in his sights the animal looked casually away, giving him a piece of neck.

"Meow," Buddy crooned, "mm-row-w-w."

The cat looked. Its working eye was a perfect circle, rimmed opal. Suddenly suspicion dawned in the cat; not a strand of fur moved, but a cold clarity, as if from without, stiffened the forms in the vicinity of the rifle sight; the flat nose and clumsy asymmetric cheeks crystallized in the air of Buddy's vision. With a sensation of prolonged growing sweetness Buddy squeezed the trigger. The report disappointed him, a mere slap, it seemed in his ears, and very local.

If his target had been a bottle, liquid wouldn't have spilled more quickly from it than life from the cat. The animal dropped without a shudder. Buddy snapped back the bolt; the dainty gold cartridge spun away, and the gun exhaled a faint acrid perfume. Buddy thought, *If he had made the river, the secret would be in enemy hands.* Going up to the slack body he insolently toed it over, annoyed not to see a bullet-hole in the skull. Chips of wood adhered to the pale fluff of the long belly. The bullet had entered the chin and passed through to the heart. Buddy couldn't imagine how he had missed by so much. Defective weapons, sabotage.

THE SOUND so small to Buddy echoed around the grounds, its loudness varying from place to place, causing curiosity where it was heard. Ted, who had backed around and aimed his truck the best he could toward the narrow gap in the east wall, wondered about it but didn't ask any of the old people for an explanation. The less he had to do with them, the better. The crowd they made rattled him. A few were outside the wall, near his front tires; the rest had bunched inside, leaving a lane between them for his truck. As soon as he had started up the motor they had fallen into position respectfully, as if what they were about to see was a great feat, a modern miracle. Dirt-face hovered near the cab, whisking back and forth with the maneuvers of the truck, flirting with the giant wheels that could crush him.

The gunshot suggested to Ted that he should hurry. The pack of Mexican cigarettes squaring out his shirt pocket and the graceful look of his own hand on the wheel were reassuring reminders of the world waiting for him. His truck was still at a slight angle to the opening, but if he went forward in first once more they would get the idea he couldn't drive at all. On the left side he had enough room: six inches. On the other side there was a thin mirror, but the sleek shape of these new GM trucks left a percentage of guesswork in estimating clearance. Ted had found, in driving, though, that you always had a little more room than you thought you did. "Plenty of room," Dirt-face said, "what's the matter? Foot freeze? Shall I climb the f. in there and do it for you?"

Ted pushed the reverse switch and delicately pressed the accelerator. "Straighten the wheels, kid. Straighten up and you're in." Ted had learned on an old hand-shift truck; automatic transmissions had the one defect of maintaining a certain minimum speed or stalling. It would make him a fool to stall in front of this mob. "More," Dirt-face called, "more." Halfway through a faint rumbling developed on the right side, where Ted couldn't see. Just grazing. Ted corrected the direction of the front wheels, while the murmuring motor maintained a creeping backwards direction. The scraping sound intensified, but a foot or two further and the body of the truck would be safely through. With a perceptible pang of release the body eased through, and a rock clattered on the running board of the cab.

As those watching on the right side could see, the slow pressure of the metal wall had caused cracks to race through the old brown mortar, mostly water and sand, and a coherent wedge-shaped section, perhaps eight feet long, collapsed, spilling stones over the grass. "Jesus Christ, kid," Gregg screamed, "you better give up. You're nuts!" The destruction was principally on the inner side. For the wall, so thick and substantial, was really two shells: what surprised the people standing in silence was that the old masons had filled the center with uncemented rubble, slivers of rock and smooth fieldstones that now tumbled out resistlessly.

THE TRUCK had pulled up while Conner was climbing the stairs; the subsequent quick clatter and soft rumble of the collapse did not reach the cupola. Buddy's rifle shot had sounded in here like a twig snapping. Conner had no regrets about ordering the animal killed. He wanted things *clean;* the world needed renewal, and this was a time of history when there were no cleansing wars or sweeping purges, when reform was slow, and decayed things were allowed to stand and rot themselves away. It was a vegetable world. Its theory was organic: perhaps old institutions in their dying could make fertile the chemical earth. So the gunshot ringing out, though a discord, pleased the rebel in Conner, the idealist, anxious to make space for the crystalline erections that in his heart he felt certain would arise, once his old people were gone. For the individual cat itself he felt nothing but sorrow.

Given his post, he had accepted it. Irishly, he had hoped for something dramatic, but the administration of order had few dramatic departments. The modern world afforded few opportunities for zeal anywhere. In the beginning there had been Mendelssohn's mess to set right: the west wing was converted into a decent hospital; Dr. Angelo was begged from Health and Medicine; there had been painting and building and bustle the first summer, and into the winter. But

over two years had passed; this was his third fair.
Many of those who had greeted him here (how as-
siduously he had attempted to learn the names of that
first batch!) were gone now, but the population of
the place had grown and was growing. There were
rational causes: lengthened lives, smaller domiciles,
the break-up, with traditional religion, of the family.
The pamphlets and pronunciamentos he daily received in the mail, from official, semi-official, and un-
official bureaus, made it clear and reasonable. Swelling poorhouses had a necessary place in the grand
process of Settling—an increasingly common term
that covered the international stalemate, the general
economic equality, the population shifts to the "vac-
uum states," and the well-publicized physical theory
of entropia, the tendency of the universe toward
eventual homogeneity, each fleck of energy settled
in seventy cubic miles of otherwise vacant space.
This end was inevitable, no new cause for hetero-
geneity being foreseen.

Despite these assurances, however, the limits of
being a poorhouse prefect chafed a man dedicated to
a dynamic vision: that of Man living healthy and un-
afraid beneath blank skies, "integrated," as the accepted phrase had it, "with his fulfilled possibilities."
Conner was bored. He yearned for some chance to
be proven; he envied the first rationalists their mar-
tyrdoms and the first reformers their dragons of reaction and selfishness. Two years remained before automatic promotion. The chief trouble with the job
was the idleness; not merely that there was so little
to do, and that he had to make work, concocting
schemes like tagging chairs, but that idleness became

his way of life. He was infected with the repose that was only suitable to inmates waiting out their days.

The very way, for instance, he had rather enjoyed the balm of standing by Hook's side for those moments this morning. Or the way he stood by this window content to gaze at nothing, or what amounted to nothing—the red-tin roof of the west wing, the sheds and pig buildings below, segments of west wall showing in the intervals between trees, and the little gate to Andrews, unlocked today for the fair. Someone was passing through, tacking from wall to bush: Lucas. He was sure it was Lucas, even from this distance. He was carrying something in a small paper bag, too big for candy, too small for food. While Conner was trying to make it out Lucas passed from sight beneath the guttered edge of the red roof.

On the glossy varnish of the window sill the canted pane of glass installed to minimize drafts laid a peculiar patina, a hard pale color neither brown nor blue.

Conner had chosen to stand by the west window because the spectacle of preparation on the east lawn scratched his eyes; he didn't wish to be made to feel again that he should go down and play shepherd. Buddy was with them; little could go wrong. It was futile anyway; the coming rain cancelled everything. The western sector of the sky was as yet unclouded. Between the tops of the trees and the upper edge of his window oblivious blue held the firmament. Then a cumbersome tumble and crash resounded, and Conner witnessed an appearance of the phenomenon which two millenia before had convinced the poet Horace that gods do exist: thunder from a clear sky.

DOWN FRONT Buddy was arranging with Ted that Pepsi-Cola would pay for repairing the wall—there was no cause for tears. Everybody had insurance. As he could see, the wall was rotten anyway. Buddy, dropping the shovel with which he had not yet begun to dig, had rushed to the accident and found its perpetrator oddly child-like. In a voice husky with apprehension the boy insisted that it had not been his fault and that he had to get to Newark in a matter of minutes or lose his job. The driver was rather handsome, in the rococo lower-class style, and Buddy instantly began to mother his innocence. The two young men were about the same height and complexion. An old man coming late to the confusion imagined at a distance that here was Buddy's twin, visiting. Buddy in fact was more highly colored, five years older, and educated. Consciously superior but distinctly tender—still elated with his outwitting the cat—Buddy helped the driver guide his truck backwards along the walk. Then the two rapidly unloaded the consignment of soft drink, rapidly because a few drops were falling, speckling the turquoise tailgate. At the thunderclap the old people scattered, gathering quilts and preserves and crude toys and canes and pieces of patient embroidery. As they hastened toward the porch, under strings of colored bulbs now swung in the air, the fourth noise of the half-hour summoned them, encouraging their flight, the ringing of the lunch signal, a tall hammered triangle used in the days of the Andrews estate to bring in the hands from the fields.

II

THEY ATE in groups of four at small square tables of synthetic white marble purchased cheaply from a cafeteria that was discarding them. The rain falling across the high windows, high from the floor, had the effect of sealing in light and noise, so the table-tops shone garishly and the voices of the old people shrilly mixed with the clash of china and steel. Mrs. Lucas was saying of her parakeet, calling really, though her companions at the table were only noses away, "Poor thing has to have some exercise, you can't ask it to sit there like a stuffed ornament, in my daughter's house it had great freedom. It can't have that freedom here, but it has to have some; its cage is too small for it, poor bird, its tail feathers stick out and it can't turn around. In my daughter's house the cat caught it and took off its tail feathers—that's the final result of all the freedom they gave it—and when they grew in, nobody thought they would, they grew too long, so the feathers stick between the bars and it can't even turn around. It can't have the freedom here it had in my daughter's house, but that's too much, not being able even to turn around. So out of simple mercy I let it out at least once in the day, in the forenoon usually. Oh she's cunning. I think it's a she, because the coloring is dull, and a male, you know, has all this brilliant plumage. I keep thinking I could clip the tail feathers with the sewing scissors but they say no, it's like taking a foot or hand off a human being, they lose their balance and don't feed and grow listless. So when I come back from baking the buns—and wasn't that futile, now that the fair's washed out—I let her out to do her tricks on the window catch and the picture frames. She even swings on the geraniums, doing her little acrobatic tricks. Oh, she's clever. If you let her out when the faucet's running she'll try to fly through it like a waterfall. Who was I to know *he'd*"—she snapped her head toward her husband, who munched slowly, because each unmeditated bite accented the soreness in his ear—"barge in right when she was on the knob with a bottle of nasty stuff in a paper bag and let the pretty little thing flutter out the door into the hall?"

"It won't go far," Lucas said.

"And then he won't even chase it. How can I chase it, with my legs?"

"We left our door open," he explained. "When it's got out before it's always come back. If you leave the door open."

"There's always the first time," she said, speaking, like him, to the other two, who acted as the channel of their argument, "and how do we know this isn't the time it will get caught fast, with its toenails? You know their toenails have to be trimmed. I didn't know that. If I had known half the trouble the bird would be I wouldn't have let her wish it on me. Anything my daughter doesn't want—she's on the move day and night, never in the same place more than a week it seems—she thinks, Oh Mom up at the Home will be glad for this. She has nothing to do. She's grateful for anything. She has nothing of her own."

"Joan doesn't think like that," Lucas explained.

"Well she didn't think twice about wishing the parakeet on us. She bought it for her boy and the boy tired of it after a week, as you might expect. So, ship it off to Mom, and let her spend her pitiful little money on fancy seed of all sorts and cuttlebone. Let her clean the cage once a day. Let her worry with the bird's nails. They're more than a half-circle and still growing. It gets on its perch and tries to move off and beats its wings and wonders why it can't, poor thing. I thought I could take my sewing scissors and trim its nails myself; they're fragile-looking; you can see the little thread of blood in there. But evidently you can't. They'll bleed unless you know just where to cut. My daughter sent along a magazine, on how to take care of them. They'll bleed if you don't know just where you can cut. So we have to wait until *he* takes it into his head to go into town with the cage to the dog doctor in Andrews. It costs money, too. It's not free. They have free medicine for humans but for any little bit of animal care you have to pay, and they call this progress. I said, you know, if you tell them you're from the poorhouse, but no, he wants to pretend he isn't."

The Lucases' companions at the table were homely Tommy Franklin, who made small baskets by filing peachstones, and Elizabeth Heinemann, a blind lady he sometimes guided about and always escorted at meals. Tommy, fearing that the other woman's hurried talk would tire Elizabeth, and anyway feeling a need to put his voice before her, began softly, "Your talking about scissors reminds me. . . ." He was so shy of talking the Lucases fell silent, to hear him, and he had to proceed. "Last month I took the bus to Burlington, to see my brother, and I noticed when I got on this old woman talking to the driver. I didn't think about it any and always try to mind my business because you never know. . . . Though I was looking out the window darned if she didn't sit down right aside of me. I guess she figured, another old person. . . . Well, she had been a nurse, she said. And she goes into this long story about how years ago she was called in to care for an old rabbi who had pneumonia. The house was full of nice things, she said, very expensive and well-kept. The rabbi's daughter kept the house. But underneath this beard, which went down to here, according to their religion, was where this terrible mess connected with his disease was, she said. She said the first thing she did was to go to the store and buy scissors, and a razor, and *shave* him. The daughter, she said, howled something terrible. And when the doctor came he took one look at the old fella and his eyes popped and he said he would never have dared to do that." Somehow when the woman had told it, this sentence was more of an ending. Tommy glanced at Elizabeth; her eyes were brilliantly fixed on a spot past his shoulder. She had a long neck stretched tall by her perfect posture; at this moment her wide mouth was broadened further by a sweet smile of expectation. Confused and inadequate, he went on. "I asked her, didn't he try to stop you, and she said, he was very sick. I guess he was unconscious when she did it. So I had to sit there listening to her tell this all the way to Burlington. Your mentioning scissors put me in mind of it." It had turned out wrong; when the woman had told the story, there had been a righteousness in her action and a kind of justice in the close. His way it sounded simply as if he were against the Jews, when he had no feelings toward them one way or another.

"I guess she thought," Lucas said, "it being a Jew, it made no difference." He studied his food, boiled potato white on the white china on the white tabletop. Potato, meatloaf and broccoli was the meal, big because this evening, if the fair were in full swing, there would be no supper. Lucas never found his appetite until dark, and after Angelo's fooling any pressure on his left gums made it ache above. Still he appreciated that Conner tried to feed them well. His thoughts predominantly were with his morning's purchase, a pint of rye, and the relations it would assume with his pain.

His wife, who during her recital had fallen behind, was eating rapidly.

Elizabeth Heinemann said, "Isn't it pretty, the rain? You never feel alone when it rains." Her clean neck elongated to bring her closer to the drumming overhead, which in the first movement of the storm was savage, though she wished it even louder, to clarify her confused inner world of tilting purple tumuli, a pre-Creational landscape fairly windowed by her eyes, the navy blue of a new baby's.

"DIDN'T I see Buddy's twin on the lawn?" an old man at another table asked.

"Buddy has no twin," Gregg said. "That's just what they say to excuse Buddy for being a moron."

"No. In a crushed-cap-like."

What the old man—Fuller—saw dawned on Gregg, and the tension of mischief smoothed the net of wrinkles on his small face. "Driving a truck?"

"I saw the truck. I didn't see him drive it." Fuller was wary of Gregg.

"How do you think he got here? Flew? You think fairies can really fly?"

"No, in a cap with his sleeves rolled up."

"Buddy's twin. He came up from Newark to see his f.ing brother. It was very touching. Gypsies had split them in the cradle. The only trouble with the twin is he got this job driving a truck and he can't drive a foot. He knocked down a big section of the wall out front."

At this point Fuller sensed that Gregg was having him on. He looked toward Hook, who he knew would speak the truth, but Hook was saying, "It was re-markable, the way the stone fence gave. You would think, now, that the few end stones would fall away and leave the rest stand. Yet a whole triangular section held together, the cracks in the mortar running in a straight line. Indeed it will cost Conner a pretty penny to have it repaired; the stone masons nowadays are used to setting nothing but bricks and the cinder blocks."

"Who was the young man I saw on the lawn then?" Fuller asked.

"Buddy's twin he means," Gregg said.

"Buddy's twin? Buddy's twin is in Ari-zona." Gregg's signals to play along were quite missed by Hook, who turned considerately to Fuller, known as soft in the head, and explained, "That young man drove the Pepsi-Cola truck here, and was nothing like Buddy. Buddy is educated."

"Educated how to be a pain in everybody's a.," Gregg said.

Fuller's broad downy eyebrows twisted a bit in perplexity. "Who was it who came from Newark, then, the driver or the twin?"

"The driver *is* the twin," Gregg said.

"The twin is in Ari-zona," Hook repeated, "in the southwest, where they are doing such wonder-ful things with irrigation."

"And who fired the shot?" Fuller asked, his soft brain affably manufacturing a third image of Buddy, this triplet holding a rifle, for he knew that around the place the only person willing and permitted to handle a gun was Buddy.

Neither Hook, whose attention at the moment had been fixed and who was incapable of receiving side impressions, nor Gregg, then buzzing around the motor of the backing truck, knew to what Fuller referred. "The kid, the twin," Gregg answered quickly, "he had a gun in his pocket. He was a tough kid. He tried to kidnap me."

"A gunshot?" Hook asked.

"Out back," Fuller said. "It was why I came outside, now that I remember."

"That wasn't a shot," Gregg told him, "that was just your own head cracking you heard." Ashamed of having said this, he stood up and added, "I'll get dessert." As the youngest and best co-ordinated of the three, it was fitting that he should. He brought back four plastic dishes of peach halves, and ate his and the extra one while his companions were still chopping theirs with spoons.

BECAUSE he had not been naturally shaped for solitude—indeed a native gregariousness had been a factor in Conner's early dedication to a social cause rather than a more vertical and selfish career, in a science or art—he felt despairing as he proceeded down the deserted stairwell and was glad to come upon Buddy, his one friend in the place. With a bang of the outer door the boy emerged into the hall, drenched. His torso beneath the soaked adhesive shirt declared its forms. The collar was recklessly open; in the V the tan hollow at the base of his throat pulsed. His face was red with exertion and his wet hair hyacinthine. "That's done," Buddy breathed, taking Conner's presence there casually. "The soft drinks are stacked under the trees by the porch. Not that we'll have anybody to drink them, except maybe Noah."

Buddy's flip acceptance of the rain, Conner's enemy, cut slightly. He asked, "Why did *you* have to handle the cases?"

"Beyond and above the call of duty," Buddy sang: parody of Conner! "The driver of the truck, a lovely youth, was so abashed by his error of smashing down our wall that he would have been incapable of completing his delivery. His impulse was to hop astride his mount and flee to Newark, where he was planning, I gathered, to deflower a local bloom."

"Smash what wall?"

"The late Mr. Andrews'. Haven't you seen? It made an audible thump."

"No I haven't. Did you get the kid's name, or were you both too excited?"

"*I* was calm as the proverbial vegetable. He was the tot. He even imagined one of the inmates—one of the smaller men—was planning to hide in his cab and make an escape. I begged him to take several, but with a tremor of his bedewed lashes he declined. Behold, his name."

Conner took the wrinkled damp piece of paper offered him, scribbled in Buddy's somewhat studied Italic hand. "What do you think he'll tell the insurance?"

"Lies, nothing but lies. He spoke pidgin Spanish in his dangerous, composed moments."

"O.K. Thanks for everything. You better change, Bedewed. What happened to the cat?"

"Cross him off your list. Our secret is safe."

"Buried?"

"Not yet. I rushed to rescue our friend Ted."

"O.K." Conner let a frown show, pettishly, since of course there hadn't been time, and he should have been on the grounds himself. "Can I see the damage from the porch?"

"Nothing easier, alas. It's no mean hole." This last was called on the fly, since the boy was running up the stairs, removing his shirt as he went.

The warm sense of shelter given by a porch whose railing is spattered with rain insufficiently offset Conner's disappointment with Buddy, his feeling that they had met at incompatible angles, and his renewed awareness that it was still the fate of his kind of man to be, save in the centers of administration, alone. The rain, falling absolutely, with an infrequent breath of wind turning a section temporarily oblique, pounded the porch rail, and a spray so fine it was more of an aroma than a mist rolled in to the wall, dampening the yellow boards, making the tops of checker tables glisten, and tinting the wicker chairs a darker vanilla. The air turned white; a fork of lightning hung above the distant orchards, shocking each spherical tree into relief. Seconds later the sound arrived. The clouds above formed a second continent, with its own horizon; a bar of old silver stretched behind the nearly tangent profiles of the farthest hills and clouds. Again lightning raced down a fault in the sky, the thunder following less tardily. On the lawn before him there was no sign of the day's celebration but the empty aligned tables and the cords of colored bulbs strung on the poles. The fumbling old men had somehow done their job.

Through veils of rain the damage was indistinct:

a discolored patch of some length, and a curious pallidity, as if the wall had been stuffed with oyster shells or fragments of plaster. It did not seem to interfere with the silhouette of the wall. While it could have been worse it was bad enough. With the shortage of craftsmen weeks would pass before a mason could be got out here. In the meantime the stones that littered the lawn should be collected. On the day of the fair the poorhouse was on view; his management would be incriminated in the apparent collapse and neglect of the wall, right where everyone entering could see. All his conscientiousness was denied by that section of stone. He hated the tongues of townspeople. A sentence from the disturbing letter of the morning recurred to him: *Yr duty is to help not hinder these old people on there way to there final Reward.* Their final reward, *this* was their final reward. How much longer before people ceased to be fools? It had taken the lemur a million years to straighten his spine. Another million would it be before the brain drained its swamp? An animal skull is a hideous thing, a trough with fangs, a crude scoop. In college, he had been appalled by the conservatism zoological charts portrayed. With what time-consuming caution had the tree-shrew's snout receded and its skull ballooned! He could picture the woman who had sent him the letter, her active pink nose, her dim fearful eyes, her pointed fingers crabbedly scraping across the paper—a tree-shrew, a rat that clings to bark. When would they all die and let the human day dawn?

He wished the rain more vehemence. In the volume of space above the lawn, set like a table for a feast, the impression was not of vacancy but of fullness; the feast was attended.

WITHIN the dining-hall most had completed dessert but few left. Where had they to go? Some days they hastened to get into the open, or gather by the television, or get to their duties. But today was what weather could not change, a holiday. They remained seated at the small white tables, enjoying the corporate existence created by the common misfortune of having their fair washed away. "Now in all Mendelssohn's years," Hook stated, "I don't recall inclement weather on a fair day."

"That bastard Conner's afraid to show his face," Gregg said. "Why doesn't he come eat the garbage he gives the rest of us?"

"Can't you picture Mendelssohn now?" Amy Mortis asked at another table. "How he'd have us all singing and shouting prayers and telling us how we all must die? Ah wasn't he the man?"

"Yet we'll see him again," the woman beside her reminded.

They were seeing him now. A great many eyes had lifted from their food and were directed by common impulse toward the vacant dais where the prefect had had his table before Conner came and deemed it arrogant to eat elevated above the inmates. These eyes conjured there the figure of the darkly dressed stocky man with spindly bird legs, nodding his large head with the great nostrils in the lean nose and the eyes pink-rimmed as if on the verge of weeping, and they were again seated at the wooden tables now on the lawn, eating in long rows on cracked and various plates, and afterwards singing in unison, "She'll be coming round the mountain" and then "Onward Christian soldiers marching as to war" and then "With arms wide open He'll pardon you." As the songs grew more religious the rims of Mendelssohn's eyes grew redder, and he was dabbing at his cheeks with the huge handkerchief he always carried and was saying, in the splendid calm voice that carried to the farthest corner and to the dullest ear, how here they all lived close to death, which cast a shadow over even their gaiety, and for him to hear them sing was an experience in which joy and grief were so mixed laughter and tears battled for control of his face; here they lived with Death at their sides, the third participant in every conversation, the other guest at every meal,—and even he, yes even he—but no. Today was not the day for talk of bad health. As the Preacher saith, To every thing there is a season, and a time to every purpose under Heaven. This was the day intended for rejoicing. Though for the moment the rain had obscured the rays of the sun, in another hour these rays would break forth again in the glory of their strength and from all the points of the compass people in the prime of their lives, carrying children in their arms, would come to this famous fair.

Conner, who entered the room at the side, had in nearly three years become enough attuned to his wards to perceive in the silence and the one direction of the heads the ghost posturing on the dais; he took a tray up to the counter with his head slightly bowed, in the manner of a man, however insolent, who arrives late at the theatre.

Conversation commenced. The live prefect displaced the dead. Buddy, entering in a crisp shirt and with his damp hair combed flat, blinked at the clatter; one vast bright beast seemed contained in an acoustic cage. The old people began to stand and leave; Buddy and Conner would be left to finish their meal in a nearly deserted room, while the kitchen help, youngsters and matrons from the town of Andrews, waited sarcastically for these last dirty plates to be handed in. Many reported to work at noon, so the kitchen smelled of raincoats.

GREGG overtook Lucas at the spot where Conner and Buddy had met a half-hour before. An oblong of water still stained the crimson linoleum, worn brown where people walked. "Where the hell have you been all goddam morning?" Gregg asked. "Conner make you his Garbage Supervisor?"

"I went in town." Lucas's lower lip, shaped like one of those rare berries that is in fact two grafted together, protruded defiantly. He liked Gregg less and less, Gregg who had never known family, who had never had a woman take the best half of the bed, who still lived in a boy's irresponsible world.

A coward in the face of blunt hostility, Gregg modified his tone. "What did he say about the tags?"

"He said it was for our good."

"S. he did. When that pansy gives a thought to my good I'll be a bag of fertilizer."

"It was interesting to see how his mind works. He said some of the women complained for their husbands who couldn't get a chair when they came in from the fields. So he thought he'd put these tags on and make every chair somebody in particular's."

"God, what a birdbrain story. He's even a bigger nut than Mendelssohn with his singing hymns. Christ, we get the rock bottom here."

"Then he made me go to the west wing, when I hadn't complained, and Angelo jabbed at my ear until I won't be surprised if I go deaf."

"I hope you do. Then sue the s. out of them. You know what I thought? I fetched a cat into the yard this morning, and what we should do is take off the tags and make a collar for the cat—it's a hell of a sick cat, dead on its feet damn near—and sneak the cat up into Conner's office. He's scared s.less of the cat anyway; I was talking to him this morning."

"*You* were talking to him?"

"Why not? Hell, he came down nosepoking and I went up to him and said, Look out the cat don't eat you, Conner. Listen. I said, This place is full of wild beasts, Conner, bears and tigers as big as your swollen head. You should have seen him stare."

Lucas smiled. "And he didn't say anything?"

"Now what could he say? He's not my boss. Nobody's my f.ing boss here. You think I'm lying."

"Oh, no. Lions and tigers, I believe you, Gregg."

"Bears and tigers. What'd you go into town for?"

"When?"

"This morning, you said you went into town. Lucas, you're slippery. You look slippery and you are."

Wanting to hit Gregg back, Lucas picked up the

handiest weapon, his favorite, the truth. "I went in to get a bottle of rye. Angelo gave me the idea."

"Screw, you didn't."

"Screw I did. I have money. I do a little work around here."

"Being a pig's friend you do. So: Marty's little boy buys a bottle of rye."

Lucas's brain, had not the dull earache been occupying the best part of it, would have ordered his body to walk away, because Gregg's jealousy was driving his tongue beyond all reasonable bounds.

"So: the pig-feeder and the bird-keeper are going to set down in their nice little cozy room with all the holy pictures and get a load on. Son of a bitch if that isn't a picture."

"Martha won't touch it," Lucas said, meaning to show how he operated on his own initiative.

But the sound of the remark was so feeble Gregg laughed delightedly, with genuine good humor. "Well then, share it with me. And some others I can get hold of. Where is it?"

"In my room."

"We'll see you on the porch. Nobody will be sitting out in the rain. I'll steal a cup. Come on, we'll make a holiday out of this f.ing mess yet. Come on."

The image Angelo had planted in Lucas's mind had been that of several men drinking together on the grass behind the wall, which was unfeasible due to the rain, so he agreed.

HOOK made haste to be among the first to enter their common sitting room, Andrews' old living-room, furnished in black leather and equipped with a vast cold fireplace. On the central round table he knew the newspaper that the noon mail had delivered would be placed. It was there for him. Many of those who would have coveted it had gone into the smaller room on the other side of the hall, where the mail rack stood, to see what letters had come. Hook had this advantage: there was no one alive in the world who would write him a letter.

He settled on the sofa and unfolded the paper to the obituary page. After perusing these unfamiliar names he revolved the paper to the opposite page, where the editorial opinions were found. The chief one was titled "Two Horns of the Canadian Dilemma."

What shall be done about overweening Montreal? Public opinion is rising hysterically against our neighbor to the north. Two months ago the Dominion was pointedly excluded from any of the chairmanships of the Free Hemisphere conference held at Tampa. The increasingly austral orientation of our policymakers is mirrored by hatred voiced on every street corner against the Old Lady of the North. Now if ever is the time for level-headed review and reassessment of the causes and factors which have led up to the Canadian imbroglio at present facing our policymakers.

The St. Lawrence Seaway, less than a year away from its china anniversary, created a new Mediterranean Sea in the nation's heartland. The Great Lake ports of Chicago, Detroit, Duluth, and others proudly expanded to fit their new role of oceanic ports. Despite the warnings of Eastern manufacturers Washington took no steps to discourage the precipitous shift of the nation's economic fulcrum from its traditional position in the Northeast— a shift that did incalculable long-range harm to New Jersey industry and shipping. Montreal bided her time. Not until the commitment of capital and manpower was irrevocable—and here is proof of the thorough-going cynicism of her motives—did our courteous neighbor to the north apply her strangle-hold. In the last six years tolls on the St. Lawrence locks have *more than quadrupled*. The American Midwest has woken and discovered itself locked in the humiliating relationship Paraguay in South America has for centuries endured in relation to Argentina, astride its sole artery to the sea. At the moment of writing it costs more to ship a ton of Nebraska grain from Chicago than from San Francisco, through the Panama Canal, to Europe!

The Canadian dilemma must be understood as having two horns. On the one hand

Hook had difficulty reading this. The light coming in the windows behind him was gravely muted by the weather, and he had to hold the paper to one side, to avoid the yellow shadow of his head; his face was tilted far back awkwardly so he would get the benefit of his bifocals. His attention moved to the political cartoon. An elderly lady, wrapped in shawls labelled CANADA, hypocritically smiled as she twisted Uncle Sam's arm, which was spiralled as tightly as a rope. Tears flew from his face. The caption was, "Don't Worry, Sam, We'll Get Those Kinks Out Yet!"

Hook folded the paper horizontally and laid it on his knees. Immaculately he interlaced his fingers and laid them on his abdomen, which sloped comfortably as he relaxed into the sofa's inclination. His eyes rested on the drawing of the old lady and she seemed very pleasant in her animation. Without forethought his consciousness faded and he slipped into sleep.

MARTHA had come to the room ahead of him. "No bird," she said, "No little bird." She was sitting on the bed, her lap spread disconsolately; all her public talk-ativeness (he knew her better than that) had faded away.

He looked automatically for a sign of green life in the thinspun cage, the delicate door of which stood ajar. The little white bath, like a miniature saltlick, held a silent eye of water. The rain outside, steadily filming the panes of the room's one window, seemed to call to this eye. "I don't know what we can do," Lucas said.

"I know it's stuck somewhere. Its claws made nearly a full circle: *why* couldn't you have taken the poor thing in town?"

"Now Martha. Do you imagine someone trims the nails of the bird in the jungle?"

"That's the jungle. When you take them out of the jungle you become responsible."

"Well, I'll look around the halls."

"Oh my poor legs."

"Here." He went to the bed, plumped out the pillow, then took his wife's ankles and, operating gently against the slight protest of her body, lifted her legs to the bed, so her head fell back into the pillow. She stared at the ceiling.

"On my feet all morning making those buns that now can't be sold," she said.

He took the thin coverlet at the foot of the bed, unfolded it, and dropped it over her, saying, "The room's damp."

"It's the sudden drop in temperature," she agreed. "The twinges I can stand, but this constant dull ache. . . ."

"Close your eyes," he said, "and when you open them, see what's in the cage."

"No letter from Joan," she said with her eyes closed.

On the way out he lifted the bottle from the bureau lightly, not wanting the paper bag to rustle. In the hall he hid it in a niche, behind a statuette of a woman whose thighs swelled through a wet nightgown. One of her hands floated in the air and the fingertips of the other touched one hip. The cylinder her bare feet posed upon was plastered into the bottom of the niche, so she had never been removed, though the mantle of dust on her shoulders had grown black. The patches of dirt the upward-tending planes of the face had received, contrasted with the bright white of the sheltered spots—eyes, and beneath the nose and the lips—gave her a clownish anxious aspect independent of the modelling.

The parakeet must have gone to the left, for to the right, after three doors, there was a dead end, a window laced with chicken wire that could with great effort be opened onto a fire escape. The window and escape were Conner's innovation; in Mendelssohn's day they would have burned.

This was the third floor. To the left Lucas travelled down a bleached corridor, and came to a crossing, four staring corners sharp as knives. One wall still bore ancient medallion wallpaper; the rest were spray-painted ivory. He looked to his right, and there, fluttering at another window of wire and glass, was the parakeet, a dipping arc of green nearly black against the luminous color of the rain.

Lucas approached lightly but before he got very

close the bird, of its own volition rather than from an awareness of being chased, darted to the right again, down another hall. By the time Lucas reached the end of this hall the bird had vanished. The channels of wood and plaster were again meaningless. The corridor the parakeet must logically have flown down had windows on the right and vibrated with shadows of the downpour outside. This row of windows gave the effect of a ship, an enclosed promenade; the clammy light fell through still air, free of dust, as at sea. He softly walked down the hall, next to the skin of the house; down below, the roofs and foreshortened fronts of some outbuildings were visible. Through the door of one shed he could see the rug of straw spread in there, dry. The radiators beneath the windows were heating; fog crept up the lower panes. To his left the successive doors were closed; occasional thin cracks revealed flecks of paint and cloth and dead matter. The corridor led to the stairway. Lucas with circumspection moved around in front of the stairs; in his stealth he felt enormously thick, cosmically big: his shoulders were Jupiter and Saturn.

The action of his feet became unconscious; the stately mass of the upward staircase passed in front of him and to his left. He stopped short, his coarse breathing suspended. On a steel bannister on the fourth floor the bird roosted fussily, shifting its awkward feet on the too broad perch and fanning its wings for balance. The bird was so small Lucas fitfully lost sight of its green in the multiplication of planes created by looking up the stairwell diagonally. Then it flickered, and with a whir mounted the terrible volume below it; hung there angrily, not so much beating its wings as shaking them in a tantrum, above Lucas, who stared beseechingly at the spinning pale belly, even stretching out his hands, to attempt to catch the bird as it fell. The parakeet folded its wings and dipped between Lucas's head and the leaning edge of olive iron beneath the stairs, veered down another corridor, and with an abrupt backwards motion, landed, and like any small gentleman walked through a waiting open door.

Desperate, yet convinced that in minutes it would be over, Lucas ran down the hall, so unused to running he ran crooked, his shoulder roughly brushing the wall. This was the west wing. He had marked the door where the parakeet had entered and threw it open. On a white bed beneath white sheets a sunken invalid lay, dreamy with heavy injections, the sheet falling away where the legs should have braced it. The parakeet was perched on the foot of the bed.

THE GREEN FLOWER had sprouted unsurprisingly; the appearance of a bear seemed to follow from that. Now the bear growled. It seemed sorry for something, but then he was sorry too, and though there was no need to say so he smiled. The bear pointed; the flower leaped; the flower skimmed over the ceiling, and at a command from the bear the door closed sharply, saying "Idiot." The bear lifted its black arms and sank from view, and the flower bloomed on the bed, its bright eye frightening. He was glad when the bear came again. A chair fell lazily, and the bear was of course sorry about that, and ashamed. Then the bear grew very clever and plucked the green flower from a picture on the wall. He was so proud, he tried to show it, but of course if he opened his his hands too wide the flower would leap again. It occurred to him that it all had been arranged to amuse him, and he laughed obligingly, so they would not feel sorry, and continued laughing when they had gone through the door, for them to hear, though curiously he was not sorry when they had left him alone again.

DOWNSTAIRS the strange thing was Conner's entry into the sitting room. He himself felt the strangeness keenly; it was a criticism of him. When the dining-hall had emptied quickly after his arrival, Buddy's chatter had grated unfeelingly on his sense that in two and a half years he had quite failed to get himself across to these people. And he felt, important within him, something he should get across, a message more momentous than his desire to be their friend, "friend" being perhaps less the word than "guide." So he courageously decided, today being a dislocated day anyway, to join them sociably. There was in his decision a shadow of the supposition that Mendelssohn—so much in the air since the rain began—would have done so. Once, however, in the room where he knew they tended to gather, he hesitated; the old people were grouped in the sofa and the chairs by the window, and a conversation held their interest. Only Mary Jamiesson noticed that he had entered. The surprise her face showed him made it harder for him to declare himself; tightened the screw on his silence.

Hook was saying in a speechifying manner, ". . . received money from the hands of the northern manufactur-ers. Now that was what was said in my father's day."

"Look at an old penny, John," Amy Mortis said, "the next time you have one. That's the face of no grafter."

"Hav-ing your face on coinage," was the considered reply, "doesn't make an honest man. Else why would we hold the opinion we do of the Emperor Nero?"

Hook tilted his cigar with satisfaction at himself. His antagonist's goiter shook as she made a crude counterthrust. "You don't think then he should have freed the slaves? You think the slaves should still be that way?"

"Ah, they still were. Had the northern manufacturers been half so concerned with the slaves in their own mills as they were with those in the fields of the South, they would have had no need to make the war for the sake of munitions profits. But they were jealous. Their hearts were consumed by envy. They had taken a beating in the Panic of '57. The civili-zation of the south menaced their pocketbooks. So as is the way with the mon-ied minority they hired a lawyer to do their dirty work, Lincoln."

"They should have kept the niggers down then?" Amy said, restating her charge, with the implication that it had been evaded by the old debater.

Conner conceived of a way to postpone inserting himself into their circle. The room was damp and chilled by the change of weather. None of the inmates had thought to light a fire, though dry wood was stacked pyramidally by the great fireplace, a black carven thing shipped from Bavaria by Mrs. Andrews, as fruit of a flighty excursion. All he needed to light a fire was paper. He moved about, with only Mary Jamiesson studying him, searching; accustomed to his office, he was bewildered that a room could contain so little paper. In a dark corner he did find, meticulously stacked on a table, some copies of a monthly publication of the Lutheran diocese titled *Sweet Charity*, forwarded to a male pensioner who had died the previous year in the west wing and to whom this musty stack appeared to form a monument. Conner took several of these white magazines and crumpled them.

"Not *down*," Hook said, "but not everywhichway either. Where do you think the freed negro was to find work, if not on the home plantation? Now did the manufac-turers want him in the northern cities? Now if I may have a minute of your time, good lady, endure this old fella for the length of one anecdote. Rafe Beam, my father's hired man when I was a boy on my father's farm ten miles this side of the Delaware, came from Pennsylvan-i-a, and had been raised near a settlement of the Quakers. The Quakers among the city dwellers had a great repu-tation for good works, and in Buchanan's day were much lauded for passing the runaway slaves on up to Canada. Ah. But the truth of it was, this old fella who was the patriarch of the sect would harbor the negroes in the summer, when they would work his fields for nothing, and then when the cold weather came, and the crops were in, he would turn them out, when they had never known a winter before. One black man balked, you know, and the old fella standing on the doorstep said so sharp: 'Dost thou not hear thy Master calleth thee?'"

Everyone laughed; Hook was an expert mimic. The hiss of avarice and the high-pitched musical fluting of the hypocrite had been rebuilt in their midst, and Hook's face had submitted to a marvellous transformation, the upper lip curling back in fury, then stiffening to go with the sanctimony of the arched eyebrows. Smiling a bit himself, he pulled on his cigar and concluded, "And no doubt he was a fair specimen of those so desirous to aid the negro."

It puzzled Conner to overhear such lively discussions of dead issues. The opposition of Republican and Democrat had been unreal since the Republican administrations of a generation ago. The word "negro" itself was quaint. Dark-skinned people dominated the arts and popular culture; intermarriage was fashionable, psychologists encouraged it; the color bar had quite melted in all states save Virginia. The Enforced Reforms, so stirring to Conner's youth, might never have occurred, to hear Hook talk.

Silently Conner laid the paper and logs and applied a match. He pictured his presence being at last revealed by a triumphant burst of flame. The glossy stock of *Sweet Charity* burned reluctantly, however, and the dark oily smoke slithering from the air spaces between the logs persisted in curling into the room. After a minute flames were visible and it became clear the chimney would not draw; the flue was closed. In a hurry Conner poked his head into the fireplace, looking for a catch, and as rapidly withdrew it, at the scent of singed hair. The lever must be on the surface of the fireplace. There seemed to be only carved bear-heads and scrolls and cherubs dotted all over with highlights. Mistrusting his eyes, his hands flittered across the black craggy surface, cold as marble.

"Buchanan, I suppose," Mrs. Mortis said, "was doing a first-rate job, eh John?"

"A ver-y unfairly esti-mated man," Hook slowly replied. "The last of the presidents who truly represented the *en*tire country; after him the southern states were slaves to Boston, as surely as Alaska. Buchanan, you know, had been the ambassador to Russia, and was very well thought-of there."

A small man with broad eyebrows, whose name, Conner believed, was Fuller, came over softly and whispered, "I think this does something." He touched a short chain hanging from the mouth of a bear, and Conner roughly pulled it. For a moment the fire continued sluggish and smoky, then the draft caught; with a jerk the smoke whipped inward, and the dry logs roared. "Birch," Fuller said, "has its own smell don't it?"

"Where is that smoke?" Amy Mortis asked aloud.

"We've built a fire," Fuller said before Conner could himself speak.

Conner wondered if the man knew who he was, that he should presume to protect him. But if he did not know who he was, why come to his rescue with the flue? All the eyes in the circle except Hook's and a blind woman's focused on him. He knew he should speak and took a breath to begin.

Staring at a beam of the ceiling, Hook announced further variations in his argument. "The panic of 1857 and not the negro lay behind the attack on the south. When the shooting died the negro became merely a cause for pecu–lation. The administration of Lincoln's man Grant was without a doubt the most crooked the nation had seen until the other Republican, Harding, came to power. Now he was around in my time: a man you would have thought dirt wouldn't cling to, as tall as a church door, and trimmed like Moses . . ."

"Well you can't blame Lincoln for Grant," Mrs. Mortis said.

Hook's mustache broadened humorously. "They were as close as Baal and Mammon," he said. "Lincoln was no lover of morals. In private practice he was an atheist, you know."

"A Deist, wasn't he?" Conner said. "A Unitarian."

"Is Mr. Conner with us?" Elizabeth Heinemann cried beautifully, turning her head on her slender neck pathetically, as if she could see.

"Yes, dear," Mary Jamiesson said, "he's been building us a fire."

"I heard that someone was. Thank you, Mr. Conner."

"Thank you," Tommy Franklin echoed, and further murmurs sounded.

"You're quite welcome—I, I'm sorry that this rain has delayed the fair."

"It's not your doing," Mrs. Mortis said.

"You can't take the world on your shoulders," the blind woman told him.

"I can't?" Conner wondered, impressed that she should phrase it so.

Mrs. Mortis, acting slightly deliberate, as if her host's small boy had wandered unbidden into the room and it was not in her place to question his presence, continued to Hook, "Well, when I get up to the Good Place, I'll have Lincoln and your friend Buchanan stand side by side a minute and we'll see who has the longer wings."

Hook did not reply, merely smiled and let his chin lapse humbly on his chest. With Conner there, his manner stated, discretion was most politic.

Whereas his presence, Conner felt, excited Elizabeth. "What else will you do, Amy?" she asked after a pause; her vowels were of different distinct colors, the consonants like leading in a window of stained glass.

"Do where?"

"In Heaven. I don't think you were quite serious before."

"Not? Well you can think what you please. It's your right."

Elizabeth's voice rose in volume and she turned her head. "Do you think, Mr. Conner—is he still here?"

"Yes, I'm here." He was standing behind her; there was no handy chair to sit in, and it seemed to be assumed he would not be with them long enough to make fetching a chair worth the trouble.

"Do you think in the Afterlife we shall *see?*"

As the pause lengthened he realized that they *did* respect him; as up-to-date where they were old-fashioned, as educated where they were ignorant. Mute, they were looking to him now, for something which was, whatever it was, not the answer he must in honesty give. False solace must be destroyed before true solace can be offered. "I can't, for myself, believe it;

vision is a function of the eyes, and when they are
gone it must follow."

"Don't be afraid," Elizabeth said, smiling broadly,
"of shocking us; this is America where, as Amy says,
we're all entitled to our own beliefs. I *agree* with you.
As a little girl I thought of Heaven as a place where I
should see, but I'm no longer a little girl. I'm a woman
old enough to have some wisdom, though of course
an old woman's wisdom can't be compared to yours,
Mr. Conner—or yours, Mr. Hook."

"I know noth-ing," Hook protested.

"As a little girl," Elizabeth Heinemann continued
after waiting a moment for Conner also to offer a remark, "I believed that everything on earth would be
in Heaven, right down to my mother's knitting needles and a pin cushion that was shaped like a pumpkin.
I saw these things in a blurred way all my childhood
and then very intensely in the weeks after my last
operation, before all the work the doctors had done
slipped away, just failed to hold, and there was no
hope left. Well! Elizabeth! Why are you going on
about yourself?" Though she made these exclamations, it was with an eerie evenness of tone. Perhaps,
long handicapped in the human game of response and
reaction, she had lost interest in it; there was a smooth-
ness in the discharge of her inner accumulations that
compelled the silence sacred performances ask. Conner, standing near and above her head, loved this
woman somewhat, for her external beauty, to the extent that the total innerness of her life did not repel
him; and he regretted it when she, feeling in the silence
of the others consent to go on, turned to him in voice

and asked, "Mr. Conner, do you have a picture of Heaven?"

"No, I'm afraid I don't really have a picture."

"I don't *either*. I no longer know what color was, or what oblong means. And it doesn't matter, it doesn't matter," she insisted, nodding her head reproachfully on the stem of her neck and vividly smiling at a spot between Hook and Mary Jamiesson. "The things you see, are to me composed of how they feel when I touch them, and the sounds they make, for everything has a sound, even silent things; when I draw near an object it says 'yes' before I touch it, and walking down a corridor the walls say 'yes, yes' and I know where they are and walk between them. They lead me, truly. At first, when this sense began to grow, I was afraid to have these voices come into my darkness; this was before I had forgotten what darkness was, when I still remembered the light. You see, I could hear the walls talking, but didn't understand that they said, 'Don't be afraid, Elizabeth; I'm here, yes,' like Mr. Conner speaking a moment ago. I believe"—her voice rose a little out of control, and dropped modestly, and in that fraction of a second Conner had time to grieve for the tremblings of her mind, these shy hallucinations which, had only the universe been made by men, would have been true evidence instead of what they were, cartoons projected on a waterfall—"we live in a house with a few windows, and when we die we move into the open air, and Heaven will be, how can I say, a *mist* of all the joy sensations have given us. Perfumes, and children speaking, and cloth on our skin, hungers satisfied as soon as we have them. Other souls will make themselves known like drops of water touching our arms.

"Living here, where there is no cause to be jealous —for don't you believe jealousy is the one *real* sin?— I've learned how sweet a human presence is, how timid, and safe. Yet when I could see, as a girl, I hated people—hated them terribly. They could run without tripping, and eat their food without spilling—my own eating was so unpleasant, I imagined, for others to watch. My sister would read to me; I hated her. I believed my parents loved her and only pitied me. There were so many jokes I couldn't understand. I must have set my ears against them. I *know* I indulged my disability in order to hurt my parents. Yet when my sight fell away finally, all those busy angry patches I couldn't quite make sense of, everything changed. A voice wasn't a twisted face but something musical. I could sit in a room with my parents and feel their emotions washing my sides, and hear a thousand details in their speech they were ignorant of, and feel my being in the room turn them toward gaiety and reverence. For when I was a young girl in my teens my presence did that."

"You should not," Hook said, "take it upon yourself to de-ny possible blessings."

Tears started to her eyes at the unexpected accusation of pride and the finish of her fine voice was scratched by the emotion of her protest, "Mr. Hook, I've never denied; I've accepted everything."

"I meant," he stated slowly, "the blessings of renewed vision."

"But how can you picture Heaven and be sensible? Mr. Lincoln in wings; a kind of tabletop, with distances between everyone that you must travel like an airplane to leap? No. Isn't it absurd? Mr. Conner thinks so. What Heaven can there be for our eyes when vision separates, and judges, and marks differences for envy to seize on? Why are we taught as children to close our eyes to pray? Please.

"Years ago, when I was still troubled, I heard a minister on the radio say, 'In Heaven there are no appearances.' For that moment that man was to me the voice of God. 'In Heaven,' he said, to me, 'everyone, everyone, will be blind.' And you needn't be frightened, Amy, because I know what it is and none of you do."

It is true, Mrs. Mortis had made a gesture of indignation.

SPRAY, cast up when the heavy rain pounded the flat porch rail, glimmered as if the sun, buried high overhead, were attempting to strike rainbows off the mist. The air had grown lighter since the first announcements of thunder; the thunder had moved off slowly to the north. Gregg, who had gathered three other men with something like his own reckless and defiant temperament, was growing impatient for Lucas to arrive with the bottle. The fear that Lucas had no bottle and had lied, slippery Lucas, and that he, Billy Gregg, had collected his friends only to seem a fool and a cheat, petrified into a conviction. "This crappy rain," he cried abruptly, "will screw Conner's goddam fair at least."

One of the men, August Hay, a Philadelphia derelict who years before had been an ice cream vendor in what was then Shibe Park, laughed; he laughed at anything. His face from the side was marked chiefly by deep creases streaming from the corner of his eye across the flat of his cheek. Whereas Gregg's net of wrinkles gave the impression of caging a bright and panicked energy, Hay's seemed to witness an old collapse. His gouged skin, the tip of his nose, his lower lids, blood-pink on the inner surface, all drooped. Hay and his two companions showed no signs of impatience; they had no responsibility in the affair; the porch was as good a place as any to sit out the rain. They talked among themselves, a distance down from Gregg. They had not seen much of Gregg since he had taken to Hook's company.

"I wonder," one of them said, "when Gregg washed his face last."

"Looks bad, don't he?"

"Bad."

"Shrivelled up, like. What does he do to himself to make himself so drawn?"

"How do you sleep nights, Gregg? On your belly or back?"

August Hay laughed and the other two followed closely.

"What the hell are you talking about for Christ sake," Gregg asked, "what the hell are you sitting down there for?"

Hay laughed. "These are our chairs, Gregg. Can't we sit in our own chairs, Gregg?"

"Who the hell says they're your f.ing chairs? Conner puts goddam little tin tags on and you think you have no right to sit in any but the ones with damn tin tags."

"Whose are you sitting in?" Hay asked, and the three laughed viciously, for the chair was his own, prolonging the laughter past mirth, old street-boys tormenting the neighborhood weakling.

"Where's the booze, Gregg?" Hay pointed beyond the porch. "That's rain, Gregg. Can't drink that. Why'n'cha wash your face in it, Gregg?"

"Why don't he wash his hands?"

The water fell from the edge of the porch roof in strings; it poured off every acute angle of the ornate brackets. "Son of a bitch, son of a bitch, son of a bitch," Gregg said. "Like some bastard's drippy nose."

"Who is?" Lucas asked. He had appeared, holding the bottle in a paper bag.

"Hooray!" Hay shouted, and the other two echoed it as a joke, beating their hands on the wickerwork arms, which resounded very little.

"Where've you been, looking at the pigs?" Gregg asked Lucas, to whom he felt, nevertheless, gratitude.

"I had to catch Martha's bird," Lucas explained, glancing at the other men. He was short of breath, not only from the chase but from suspensefully putting the parakeet in the cage without waking Martha, who had been snoring under the coverlet. His palms still tingled with the sensations of holding the living bird captive in his hands. The rapid beating of the tiny breast and the strong effort of the edged wings to unfold had affected him disagreeably, even stirred queasiness, after the sight of the dying man in the bed smiling and nodding like a judge. There was something dreadful to Lucas in the thought of blood pumping through pliant, dilating vessels; he was startled whenever, inadvertently touching fingertips and thumb, he felt the shudder of his own pulse. Living flesh to him felt like food in the act of being eaten by an amorphous, carnivorous creature: life itself. For this reason he disliked touching anyone, or having them touch him. He asked Gregg, "Did you steal the cup?"

Gregg produced it: white china. "Slop it in," he ordered.

Lucas worried off the cap, held in place by a new-fangled set of wires, and, keeping the bottle dressed in the paper bag, poured a bit of liquor into the cup Gregg held, enough to cover the bottom. Before taking a sip Gregg carefully swirled the cup, and like a flexible brass coin the half-inch of liquid swayed in the white cavity. Then with some delicacy of gesture he took his swig. As in the flavor of certain vegetables acres of bland rural landscape are contained, stone houses, fields, and grassy lanes, so this rasping hard taste flowered in Gregg's mouth into high brick blank walls, streets of pocked asphalt bleeding in summer heat, the blue glint on corrugated iron where it is not rusted orange, the sun multiplied down a row of parked cars, tangerines pyramided behind plate glass, manhole covers, filth in gutters, condoms discarded on windowsills, and unpainted doorways scratched with wobbly slogans like F. THE POPE.

Gregg coughed and hawked. "Goddam Lucas, this is p. you've bought here."

"Hey, hey," the other men clamored, waving their arms but keeping their chairs.

Gregg darted off the porch into the rain and returned running with two bottles of ginger ale cooled by the rain in the cases Buddy and Ted had stacked.

"To kill the rotten taste," he explained, and they drank it this way, at the proportion of 1 to 2, out of the common cup.

"ATHE-ISM," Hook said in answer to Conner's attribution of Deism to Lincoln, "wears as many faces as Satan."

This rejoinder fell among them neglected, for Elizabeth's hopes of Heaven had disjointed their commerce awkwardly. Her own mouth tightened into a sharp, impervious expression unsuited to her, and Conner realized she had expected some sort of praise. He realized as well that Hook was attempting to offer it when he said, "No doubt, Elizabeth, Heaven will be something of what each wants it to be." But this, too, was ignored, and for the moment Conner wondered if Hook, like himself, was not excluded from a certain alliance of affection that existed among these people.

It was Tommy Franklin who at last spoke and was turned to eagerly by the blind woman.

"Well my ideas of the next place," he began, and lifted his downcast face to ask, "Did you say you wondered what other people thought?"

"Yes," she said, "please tell, everyone. I'm so interested."

"Well,"—he spoke with difficulty throughout— "I've not given it the thought you have. The last I remember thinking was as a boy of maybe fourteen, that it couldn't be in the sky. It turned out my father thought the same. He said, and he claimed he got this from the Bible, one day we'd be lifted up from our graves and Heaven would begin right here. I liked to hear that because I had always liked the section of country around our place. Then I wondered about the animals, because if we came out of the ground they might too, and I wondered where they'd go. I thought of all the stock I'd seen my folks kill, and even if we got the whole farm back, I didn't see the place for them all. And a lot of wildlife depend on eating each other, foxes and hawks to mention two, and what would they eat? I asked him, my dad, and this time he said there would only be two of each animal, a male and a female, like they came off Noah's ark. It didn't seem to be enough, but I let it go at that, and that's the last thinking I recall doing on the subject." Aware that he had disappointed Elizabeth, he scowled at his knitted fingers, nicked and red from filing peachstones.

"Rafe Beam used to recite," Hook said,

> "The animals came out two by two,
> The chipmunk, mink, and kangaroo;
> The horse came down, clippety-clop,
> And Mrs. Noah shook out her mop."

He couldn't help chuckling himself at this, a distant tickled laugh.

"All right, Tommy," Elizabeth said. "Who now? Amy? Bessie dear."

Fuller left the circle to put more logs on the waning fire Conner had built. Conner coveted his chair, for it symbolized inclusion, but he didn't intend to stay much longer; Buddy must be up in the office alone, and the boy's probable petulance tugged at Conner's official side.

"The Book says," Bessie Jamiesson said, "the rich

will be poor, and the poor rich. So I've always thought I'd be a beauty, and my mother not; but I won't let on; I'll treat her better than she treated me, when I was her girl. I expect we'll all be about the same age."

"If you lose your long jaw," Amy Mortis said, "that means my goiter goes too. And your bad eyes, Elizabeth. It's your right."

How tiny, Conner thought, this woman's head was without her bonnet. A mere egg and, as she had said, partially bald. He wondered if, technically, she was a dwarf. He wondered what the technical definition of a dwarf was.

"Mr. Conner," Elizabeth appealed, "will I be made to see?"

"I'm not really an expert on eschatology." The coldness of his voice disappointed even him.

"Please, won't you give us your ideas? They say you don't believe, but I think everyone believes, in their heart."

Conner on the contrary believed that in their hearts no one believed, which accounted for the strained, or bluff, expressions on the faces of the few clergy he had met. "I'll try to tell you"—in his earnestness he touched the blind woman on the shoulder, sharp bones at variance with her velvet appearance—"my conception of Heaven. Like Mr. Franklin, I see it placed on this earth. There will be no disease. There will be no oppression, political or economic, because the administration of power will be in the hands of those who have no hunger for power, but who are, rather, dedicated to the cause of all humanity. There will be ample leisure for recreation."

"Naked girls on the seashore," Mrs. Jamiesson interpolated.

"Leisure, and no further waste of natural resources. Cities will be planned, and clean; power will be drawn from the atom, and food from the sea. The land will recover its topsoil. The life span of the human being will be increased to that of the animals, that is, ten times the period of growth to maturity."

"More poorhouses," Mrs. Mortis said.

"There will be no poor."

"All the more reason for poorhouses; the only reason people put up with their old ones now is to get their money."

"Money too may have vanished. The state will receive what is made and give what is needed. Imagine this continent—the great cities things of beauty; squalor gone; the rivers conserved; the beauty of the landscape, conserved. No longer suffering but beauty will be worshipped. Art will mirror no longer struggle but fulfillment. Each man will know himself—without delusions, without muddle, and within the limits of that self-knowledge will construct a sane and useful life. Work and love: parks: orchards. Understand me. The factors which for ages have warped the mind of man and stunted his body will be destroyed; man will grow like a tree in the open. There will be no waste. No pain and above all no *waste*. And this heaven *will* come to *this* earth, and come soon."

Mrs. Mortis asked, "Soon enough for us?"

"Not you personally perhaps. But for your children, and your grandchildren."

"But for us ourselves?"

"No." The word hung huge in the living room, the "o" a hole that let in the cold of the void.

"Well, then," Mrs. Mortis spryly said, "to hell with it."

They all laughed, but it was Hook's laughter, because of the common exclusion from the run of human hearts that minutes before he had imagined as binding them, that wounded Conner and brought on his controlled anger.

"MR. HOOK," he said in an insistent voice, claiming the initiative, "you've laughed several times. What strikes you as amusing?"

"Now I meant no offense."

"Is it the wish to eliminate pain that strikes you as amusing?"

"Indeed not, but it is an error now to believe that the absence of evil will follow from the elimi-nation of pain."

"Pain *is* evil."

"The Roman Empire was very pros-perous, and yet evil."

"There was a good deal of pain in pagan Rome."

"Arti-ficially induced," Hook said, lifting his flattened hand edgewise, like an ax poised to cleave the chair arm. "It need not have been. The Emperor Nero, now, besides arranging exhibitions for the enter-tainment of others, had torments inflicted upon himself, to re-lieve his boredom."

"There can be mental as well as physical pain," Conner said. "I've never encountered anything I considered evil that couldn't be described as pain."

"Well, then, is your vive-section evil? And hurling animals off to perish on the moon?"

"You must understand that there is a distinction—"

"Ah; I am grateful to hear that word. Dis-tinctions, Harry Gorman, my old instructor in debate, used to say, consti-tute the anatomy of discussion. Now there are many sorts of pain. There is that which we un-dergo gratefully, such as dental work. There is that which we cause ourselves, as in war or automo-bile accidents. And there is that caused by our body in at-tempting to warn us of disease. When one reads in the paper that the state has declared war on suf-fering, these distinctions are not mentioned."

"I don't know if they're worth mentioning. All suffering comes upon the individual uninvited, and it all interferes with his fulfillment."

"Why, on the contrary, in most cases even disease is invited by trans-gressing the commandments, no-tably those against gluttony and greed. And far from opposing the existence of virtue, suffering provides the opportunity for its exercise."

Conner smiled regretfully; he saw no great good in depriving a man of what had comforted him for ninety years, yet more than his immediate authority had been insulted, and he devoutly wished to pin his antagonist against the rock that underlay his own philosophy. "I'm afraid I have little use for a virtue purchased at the price of some of the suffering I've seen."

"I read the papers," Hook said with some indigna-tion. "I have lived in the world. Now in whose shoes would you rather stand, your own as a young man certi-fied to a long career in govern-ment, or in mine, those of an old fella who has buried all his children and idly waits to be struck down any day? You have heard our blind lady speak; did she protest of injustice?"

Elizabeth brightened and said, "Oh, no: as I said, I was a very vain and fretful girl, and I tremble to think what I would have become had my sight been cured. Very quarrelsome, I'd imagine, and with *no* insights."

"And Bessie," Hook went on, "are you indig-nant, because you lacked the blessing of beauty?"

"I thank God I do," she responded. "You take my mother; she thought for being a looker the world owed her a living, and she never gave herself or anybody else around her any rest. I've had an easy life and won't be sorry to go. But my mother, the day she died, she was hopping, and gave me a cut I still carry the scar of around."

Conner began too wryly, "I wish—"

"Now in my own life," Hook said, and brought down the edge of his hand upon the chopping-block of the chair arm, "looking back I perceive a mar-vel-ous fitting together of right and wrong, like the joints the old-time carpenters used to make, before everything was manufactured metal and plastic. I was sickly as a child, and could not enjoy the sports the others did. But due to my ill health I learned to care for my body and have outlived those that were stronger by nature. The penalty I've paid for this has been burying all of my kin, until there is none living who remembers me as I was before"—and a disagreeable expression, like a lavender shadow, passed over his face—"I reached this state. But the con-solation here is, I shall be willing to die, having made the Gentleman's acquaintance before, and having sent so many ahead to welcome me. Ver-y seldom, in my life, did a transgression not bring its own punishment, so that in some cases, as drunkenness, I could not tell where the offense left off and the penalty began. And who is to say how the ailments of my childhood may have been the fruit of my father's short-comings, or of his before him."

"You believe that too?" Conner was sincerely surprised.

"Indeed and double. The bookkeeping is far more strict than even that of a Boston banker. If the size of a mouth is passed down, why not the burden of wrongdoing? Had the men so busy at tor-menting the atom busied them-selves inspecting the sins of un-fortu-nates, we would have books of the balances Providence strikes. Virtue is a solid thing, as firm and workable as wood. Your bitterness"—he looked directly at Conner, his eyes greatly magnified by cataract lenses—"is the willful work of your own heart."

"VIRTUE," Conner said, his level tone making clear that while willing to take this last, frontal attack, he now felt free to repay in kind. "How do you define virtue?"

"Virtue," Hook said, "I understand as obedience to the commands of God."

"Where do you locate these commands?"

"Why, they locate you."

"We are born with them."

"As we are born with ten fingers; they grow in strength."

"But a baby is essentially virtuous."

"Why, does a baby seem evil to you?"

"A baby seems neutral. A baby is a bundle of appetites that society, for its convenience, teaches certain restrictions. To enforce these it invokes the supernatural as a mother would an absentee father."

"He is not absen-tee."

"No? What makes you think, God exists?" As soon as he pronounced the ominous hollow noun, Conner knew absolutely he could drive the argument down to the core of shame that lay heavily in any believer's heart.

"Why, there are sever-al sorts of evidence," Hook said, as he held up one finger and then added a second, "there is what of Cre-ation I can see, and there are the inner spokesmen."

"Creation. Look at the smoke of your cigar; twisting, expanding, fading. That's the shape of Creation. You've seen, in the newspapers you've just said you read, photographs of nebulae: smears of smoke billions of miles wide. What do you make of their creation?"

"I know little of astronomy. Now a flower's creation—"

"Is also an accident."

"An ac-cident?" Hook smiled softly and he touched the fingertips together, better to give his attention.

"Lightning stirred certain acids present on the raw earth. Eventually the protein molecule occurred, and in another half-billion years the virus, and from then on it's evolution. Imagine a blind giant tossing rocks through eternity. At some point he would build a cathedral."

"It seems implaus-ible."

"It's mathematics. The amounts of time it takes is the factor that seems implausible. But the universe has endless time."

"Not according to Scripture."

"Not according to Scripture, no."

"I do not quite see how any amount of time can gener-ate something from nothing."

"Presumably there was always something. Though relatively, very little. The chief characteristic of the universe is, I would say, emptiness. There is infinitely more nothing in the universe than anything else."

"Indeed, you propose to extinguish re-ligion by measuring quantities of nothing. Now why should no matter how much nothing be imposing, when my little fingernail, by being something, is of more ac-count?"

"Yes, but there is something. Stars; many of such size that were one placed in the position of the sun we would be engulfed in flame. The issue is, can any sane mind believe that a young carpenter in Syria two thousand years ago *made* those monstrous balls of gas?"

For the first time, Hook was slow in answering. He shifted his position, and the old dry leather audibly protested. "As to being a carpenter, it has often struck me that there is no pro-fession so native to holy and constructive emotions, or so appropriate for God made flesh to assume."

"The truth is, Mr. Hook, that if the universe was made, it was made by an idiot, and an idiot crueler than Nero. There are no laws. Atoms and animals alike do only what they can't help doing. Natural history is a study of horrible things. You say you read the papers; but have you ever walked around the skeleton of a brontosaurus? Or watched microbes in a drop of water gobble each other up?"

"No, but I have seen a lobster being cooked."

"These are our fathers, Mr. Hook. Monsters. *We* are mostly monster. People speak of loving life. Life is a maniac raving in a sealed room."

"Now it has never been claimed," Hook said, "that the Creator's mind is a book open for all to read. This I do know, that that part of the uni-verse which is visible to me, as distinct from that which is related to me, is an unfailing source of consolation. Dumb creatures are more than their skeletons. Even a spider may set us a lesson. As to the stars which so repel you, they are to me the points of light arranged at random, to give the night sky adorn-ment. I have sometimes thought, had you and your kind arranged the stars, you would have set them geo-metrically, or had them spell a thought-pro-voking sentence."

Conner waved his hand impatiently. "As a student of debate you know how little humor proves. What was your second piece of evidence? Inner spokes-men? The truth here is, there is no door where these spokesmen could get in. We've sifted the body in a dozen directions, looking for a soul. Instead we've found what? A dog's bones, an ape's glands, a few quarts of sea water, a rat's nervous system, and a mind that is actually a set of electrical circuits. An ex-periment that might interest you, Mr. Hook, was con-ducted several years ago by a team of Latin-American scientists. They took a young Indian girl from the mountains of Peru who had been educated entirely by

Catholic nuns. By means of a series of precisely directed electrical shocks, administered while she was under drugs, she was induced to have a vision of Christ as real to her as I am to you."

With this he knew that he had indeed succeeded, had touched the core of shame and shaken Hook. All the old man could say was, "That was a very cruel experi-ment."

"I don't know why. The girl was ecstatic. He spoke to her in Quechua."

"He spoke?"

Conner paused. "I think the report said the appearance told her not to be afraid."

The fire had failed to take Fuller's large logs; and the rain continued more quietly outside, infrequently pattering on the ashes as a few drops found their way down the chimney. Hook was silent a moment, but might have spoken again, had not an interruption occurred. "Mr. Hook," Buddy said sharply, and he stepped forward, lithe and clean in his crisp shirt and his skin quickened by indignation. "I'll tell you my own experience with popular religion." Conner realized that, however long Buddy had been listening by the door, he did not comprehend the situation, that Conner stood among the ruins of a venerable faith; helplessly Conner perceived that in the boy's brain the grotesque idea of a rescue had taken form. "I watched a friend die," Buddy continued quickly, speaking solely to Hook. "It took a long time. His bones were riddled with cancer. Every time he'd turn over in his sleep, he would break a bone; this was toward the end; at first it was just his joints, one by one, stiffening, and not obeying. He and I were very young; we prayed. We prayed for years, yet the pain came on, and in the end we prayed simply that he die now, before the disease was through playing with him. It would have been such a little thing for God to do, yet it was not done, even that little thing. At last the doctors themselves did it, and killed my twin brother with drugs, on his fifteenth birthday."

"Why Buddy," Fuller asked, "wasn't that your brother on the lawn this morning with the bare arms?"

His manner of asking was so sincere, laughter was general.

Hook had not laughed, however, and now pronounced tiredly, "That is a ver-y terrible tale. Let an old fella say one thing more, and then he'll hold his peace. When you get to be my age—and I shall pray that you never do, I wish it on no one, but if you do—you shall know this: There is no goodness, without belief. There is nothing but busy-ness. And if you have not believed, at the end of your life you shall know you have buried your talent in the ground of this world and have nothing saved, to take into the next."

THOSE on the porch thought they were seeing things. A small red car—foreign no doubt—drove up in the rain and stopped at the break at the wall, blocking the entrance. Black snouts commenced to poke from the little windows. Ends of bulky cases, they stuck out and sneaked back, like the heads of several turtles caught in one shell. Then the doors jumped open, and six men with raincoats with blue pants showing beneath hopped out, slamming each other's doors, and raced up the path, bobbing with the effort of carrying cumbersome shapes.

The foremost and first to reach the shelter of the porch, a little one with hair parted centrally and a sharp nose, asked, "Who's in charge?" Three of the men with him were in their sixties—the biggest, and oldest, with an overbearing pious brow, carried under an orange canvas what had to be a tuba—and the other two were boys, insolent and drowsy.

"He is," August Hay said of Gregg, who quickly hid the bottle beneath the wicker chair.

"Him? In charge of what?"

Furious to have attention thrown on him, Gregg snapped, "Son of a bitch does it look like we're in charge sitting here with tags on our chairs like pigs in a zoo?"

"You're the band," Lucas told them. "Conner's probably up in his office."

"The band!" Hay crowed. "What the hell are you doing here? Look at the mob out there." He threw his hand toward the empty grass beyond the black-soaked porch rail. "Ice cream, ice cream," he began to call, "getcher red-hot ice cream heeyah."

"Bugs in his head," the leader said to his followers.

"Conner's probably in his office," Lucas repeated. "Ask inside for the stairs."

"Nobody told us not to come," the leader said, half to the men behind him and half to those in front. Conscious of this remark's weak positioning, he added with unnecessary loudness, "This is the third Wednesday of August." The ensuing silence made him appear foolish.

"Bugs in his head," August Hay explained.

As the six, in file, passed into the poorhouse proper they clicked off glances of disdain with industrial precision. The two boys, bringing up the rear, exchanged a lazy comment with the word "characters" easily audible.

The marriage Lucas had looked forward to, between the pain in his ear and the rye, had proved a mournful disappointment. The liquor dulled the pain less than the pain dulled the uplift of the liquor; in an oval area inches above the back point of his left jaw the sum of his existence, it seemed, was absorbed in the rhythm of a cautiously pulsing sponge. Pain seemed green—the green of old grass—and its absence —the penetration of the liquor—brown. Like infringing watercolors these sensations blurred into one another, one dominant and now the other, and at moments like paint over wax the slow movement brought into relief the exact shape of the small bones of his ear, three white, few-fingered, interlocking hands. His upper lip lifted in self-dislike. Perhaps, if he had obeyed Angelo and kept the matchstick out, the pain would be gone; again, if he had never seen Angelo, the pain would be sharper and not so broad and smothered in quality. Lucas felt uncommonly depressed and careless. Drunkenness, in a man like August Hay, melts the restraints on cheerfulness. On the contrary with Lucas: he kept up courage consciously. Sap his mind, and the lid was lifted from a cesspool of muddy colors.

WHILE upstairs Martha, wakened by a sweep of rain, had discovered the parakeet returned to his cage and had taken this bird onto her shoulder; each time the black-and-yellow head, striped finer than any fabric, dipped to touch its downturned beak to the blue skin beneath her eye, she sang out, "Aren't you silly? Aren't you silly?"

Such ecstasy for so small a bird to undergo!

"AND why else does anybody these days put up with old people except in the hope of getting their money when they pass on?" Amy Mortis thus concluded explaining why the world of the future would be a world of poorhouses.

Conner stood over them, hardly considering her point—that poverty alone held the generations together. His attempt at intercourse with the inmates was ending less well than it had begun. What had caused the fury of this old woman? They were all furious. Their heads were dark in their chairs, facing away from what light the windows admitted. "Poverty," he said, "isn't a positive thing; it's a lack. The scientific state adds; it takes nothing away." He stood in such an ambiguous relation to these people, between that of a shepherd and that of a captive, and his quarrel with Hook had produced such a darkness, that he spoke blindly, uncertain even of whether he lingered among them in the hope of making himself clear, or merely to avoid the appearance of a retreat. One retreat had taken place: they had withdrawn from him.

"It almost seems," Elizabeth Heinemann sighed aloud to herself, "there's to be no fair."

Like a flicker of a tail a silent stroke of dry light

whitened the room, occupying in its moment every corner, even the black mouths of the carven bear heads. "Isn't it a wonder now," Hook offered, "that so few men are struck by lightning now, compared to my day. So many were struck standing on the loaded hay wagons, coming in under a storm. Now in Matthew it speaks of lightning going from east to west, at the end." He cleared his throat and concluded, "At the beginning of the first war with the Germans it seemed the End had come, the portents were so plentiful: Halley's Comet, and the men in the trenches saw the angels overhead. Lucy had such terrible dreams." Lucy had been his second daughter, the child that had died most recently.

Buddy came whispering up to Conner, who repeated "The band?" involuntarily.

The elderly men and under their direction the two youths had removed their raincoats and hung them in a closet Buddy had showed them. Now they stood forth in creased cerulean uniforms. With double rows of chased silver buttons and brilliant braid looping and running along every seam, they glinted like seraphim in the dull light.

The shortest, whom Conner remembered from the two previous years, stepped up and said, "You should have called before this if you didn't want us to come."

"You didn't want to come?"

"It's not the point what I want. If there wasn't to be an affair because of the weather, you were obliged to notify. In all the years we've come here before there's never been rain."

"As a matter of fact," Conner said, smiling, "I did

call your home around noon, but your daughter said you were gone."

"Sure, I was gone. There's more to this job than putting on blue pants and combing my hair and getting into the car. There's a lot of managing in connection here. Rain or shine we fulfil our obligations to the letter, is the way we do it. It's always worked before."

"I respect you for it," Conner said. "I'm glad you're here," he added, seeing that this wasn't assumed.

In ones and twos more inmates were drifting from spots around the Home into the room, shuffling amusedly through the screen of uniforms drawn up like a guard. It was as if the world had been holding its breath while Hook and Conner debated its condition, and now resumed bumping onward.

The leader persisted in making himself clear. "That half of the fee given in advance, you can't get back now. We can't return it. What kind of business would that be, if we came all the way out here and then handed back your money?"

"Is this the whole band?"

"Wind ensemble. We use the term 'wind ensemble.' There's no call for marching bands any more. The parades they have now are all floats with whores on 'em advertising some soap."

"Last year, weren't there more of you?"

"Yes and twenty years ago there were twenty more. Times change, if you haven't heard. If there's a half-dozen bands like this left south of Trenton I'll be surprised. If you're worried about your money you won't have to pay for personnel you don't get. But this is the third Wednesday of August and rain or shine we expect to play and get paid. There's two more cars should be here now, if they'd listen to their orders. Young ones driving; they'll show up I guess when the mood hits 'em. What's the humor?"

Conner too did not know why he laughed, except that the wooden fixity wrought by economic concern on the other's face challenged his own to keep impossibly stiff. "Young people in cars coming," he repeated.

"That's what I said. I got 'em dressed and wiped their noses and I guess they'll turn up. Between sixteen and sixty it seems nobody can carry a tune, that's the impression you get if you try to keep a band going."

"A wind ensemble," Conner said. "I can believe it." He laughed, and laughed again when he felt Buddy beside him flinch. Buddy's mechanical generation had never learned how to laugh; Conner's own was the last that knew how. "Well, make yourselves comfortable," Conner continued. "You can dry out by the fire. Oh. The fire's gone out. Well, have some chairs. You can talk or play—" He was going to say "cards."

"Play? You want us to play our instruments?"

The idea struck Conner as remarkable. "Why not?" he said quickly. "You came here to play and get paid."

"We're short two-thirds of the parts," the leader protested.

It seemed, as Elizabeth had said, that there was to be no fair; a gust of irresponsibility had swept into the room, as if the fair were, rather than an awaited holiday, an annual humiliation from which they were this year to be delivered. The six musicians were egged on. Chairs were arranged. The instruments were unsheathed: flute, cornet, trombone, tuba, French horn, parade drum. This last was a gay thing, painted with long lozenges. Sheets of yellow music were unfolded and clipped to the instruments. Mrs. Mortis remarked to Hook how much the fella on trumpet resembled Truman, who gave away China to the Russians. Without his customary spark he countered that the tuba man was the image of Hoover, who plunged the common man into the Great Depression for the benefit of the Wall Street bears. The musicians made their instruments speak haltingly, and twisted mouthpieces and shook out moisture. Then they commenced definite tunes: marches that colored the air, dimly at first, with the colors of the flag. The weave of the orchestration was tattered and torn on the fewness of the instruments, but here the cornet placed a white star, and there the flute and drum together spread a broad red stripe, and above the heads of the men, moving minimally, a phantom banner beat. They rendered, with rising spirit, *Fairest of the Fair*, then *Hands Across the Sea*, then *On the Mall*, by E. F. Goldman, in which the teen-age flautist strangely excelled.

LUCAS had sunk into an apathy so profound that even his earache seemed a stranger. He had held no hopes, really, for his alcohol party. Gregg, who had held some, was generating a savage temper, and had established a monopoly of rye. The rain was letting up, and it seemed to Gregg that as the rain slackened his revenge on Conner was being taken from him. As a pearly light infiltrated between the upright rods of rain, which was more like a harp now and less like a massive sail filling and sagging as the wind came and went, Conner seemed to lord it over them again.

"Son of a f.ing bitch," Gregg began, "be putting tags on our necks next, and balls and chains on our feet. Fairy doesn't even have the sense of half a man. Where's that cat I sneaked in? What I'm going to do is pry every stinking tag off these f.ing chairs and make a f.ing collar and throw that cat right in Conner's puked-up face. Pale turd." He jumped from his chair and whirled to peer in the windows. "Now what the s. is that music? Who the s. says we have to have music when his goddam fair is washed out? Son of a bitch; birdbrain noise." Heedless of the diminished rain, he raced off the porch to go out back and find the cat, who must be keeping dry in one of the barns.

Like many humanists Conner was deeply responsive to music. In the language of melody speeches about man's aspirations and eventual victory could be made that explicit language would embarrass. He could not hear a dozen chords without crystals building in his head, images: naked limbs, the exact curve of the great muscle of a male thigh, cities, colored spires soaring. Man was good. There was a destination. Health could be bought. A remark of Amy Mortis's exerted a subconscious effect. He envisioned grown men and women, lightly clad, playing, on the brilliant sand of a seashore, children's games. A man threw a golden ball, his tunic slowly swirling with the exertion; a girl caught it. No fear here, no dread of time. Another man caught the girl by the waist. She had a wide belt. He held her above his head; she bent way back, her throat curved against the blue above the distant domes. The man was Conner. Then there was Conner again, at his desk, speaking to grateful delegates, calm, flexible, humorous; the listeners laughed, admiringly. Conner shunned admiration, and gained it doublefold; the world was under his wing. Yet in visualizing this world which worshipped him, he returned to the triangles and rhomboids flashingly formed by the intersection of legs and torsos scissoring in sport, and the modulated angles of nude thoracic regions, brown breasts leaning one against another, among scarves of everlasting cloth, beneath the sun.

Hook, less imaginative, tapped his toe out of respect for the patriotic content of Sousa's songs—he had witnessed many a parade to these tunes—and swiftly grew restive. Music affected him as women's talking did, when there was no interceding in it. He was an instructor, not a listener. Further he had been closeted within for three hours—he judged it was shortly after three—and now that he had been absent from him for such a time he missed his final pupil, Gregg.

He stood, whispering his intention to "give his knees a bending," words no one quite heard, though the sound drew some attention to himself, tall and stiff from his long sitting, trying to focus in the narrow beams of his sight the way out, as he made uncertain protestations with his elegant tan hands. "Let me disoblige no one; I want no more than room to die," his manner of exit declared.

"Hookie looks bad," Mrs. Mortis said to Bessie

Jamiesson, under cover of the martial music. "Conner ought to be shot, going after the old man that way."

"What did Conner want down here with us anyway?" Mrs. Jamiesson asked. "Mendelssohn never made himself common like that."

"We won't see another Mendelssohn, not in our little time."

Hook did feel slightly shaken; his discussion with the prefect had sent his blood pumping with unaccustomed force. He wished again, contemplating the distances visible from the porch, that the poor home were in sight of water. The rain was lifting; the far hills bearing the orchards glistened, existing in a washed atmosphere. Though he had thought he had noticed his piercing voice through the windows, Gregg was absent from the porch. Lucas sat in a near chair; further down the line three of the disreputable element had established themselves. "Isn't it peculiar now," he said to Lucas, "but I remember, after such a storm, how the Dela-ware would show blue before there was any blue in the sky to reflect. Now look how heavy the drops are, as their number lessens."

"It just seems so," Lucas said, covering both remarks, and unable to say more, though he bore the old man no hard feeling.

"Did you in-quire about the tags?"

"I asked this morning. He had a good reason, I forget what."

"He is a re-markably earnest man," Hook stated generously, after which he added, "I believe a demon drives him."

Gregg, damp and beside himself with shock and

fury, came onto the far end of the porch and, advancing, cried, "The goddam rotten cat, they've killed the dumb son of a bitch and let the body lie in the rain, they just let it lie! The f.heads shot it and let it lie out there, the cat I brought over the wall, they killed for no reason."

"That animal that was so sick?"

"No sicker than Conner will be when I get to him."

Hook recognized in the small man's melting eyes signs of a madness that created a hazard for them all, and the old disciplinarian showed as he said, "Why, it was better to put it out of its misery than let it linger."

"I'll kill the c.sucker. I have rights."

"No, now," Hook said, "you don't, if truth be known."

THE DAY'S RAIN lifted; the high yellow house hove clear of spray; the many gray connections between below and above were snapped. The unpainted wood of the tables was soaked black. Drop by drop the colored bulbs slipped their thin jackets of water. A few of the women ventured into the open, treading distastefully the drenched lawn in which the circular cobwebs of the grass spiders showed like mirrors left lying in the grass. The song of the birds was especially strident. Hook from the porch heard what he rarely heard, a bobolink. Mrs. Lucas came down from her room, her legs better. The musicians laid their instruments aside. The inmates of the home, already united in expectation of the holiday, had passed as a group through two turns of fortune: the rain, and the rain's abatement, which last joined them together in a mood of raucous, cruel exhilaration quite unlike the sweet and moderate expectation of the morning. Boxed within the house three hours, they retained the nature of a mob. They spoke loudly; old people who seldom conversed, being of different types, cackled together. They were like school children whose vacillating principal at last grants them an excursion which he had threatened to withhold as discipline and which he believes is a greater treat for them than it truly is.

Conner was immediately concerned with the broken wall. The litter must be removed, before any townspeople came. He hated waste and liked things clean. He was so anxious that the stones be taken from the lawn that he dared use, he hoped tactfully, his authority as prefect to assemble some of the inmates before they became involved in other tasks, or ran away. He marshalled the men in the living-room, who had witnessed his argument with Hook, and passing the porch with this troop also enlisted the five men loitering there. He exempted Hook, who was also present, as being too old for even light labor, but Hook, inquisitive, as were some of the women, came along, thereby laying the foundation for a later misunderstanding.

III

ON CONNER'S INSTRUCTIONS Lucas brought the wheelbarrow from a shed behind the west wing. The rest straggled around Conner, rather too closely, a sizeable group of men. "Whose car is this parked across the entrance?" Conner asked aloud.

"The band's," Gregg answered.

"They'll have to move it."

When Lucas came up with the wheelbarrow, Conner had him put it at the far end of the field of fallen stones, beside one of the biggest. This stone, a rough brown egg so soaked by the downpour grains of red sand rubbed off on their palms, Conner and Gregg together lifted into the metal pan of the wheelbarrow, setting it forward, where the wheel would take its weight. It was agreeable for Conner to find Gregg's shoulders beside his; he remembered chatting with him in the morning, this the man good enough to try to feed the cat. The rock settled resoundingly. Conner's fingers were nearly pinched in his inexperience. Nevertheless it gave him unexpected satisfaction, handling stones in this wet, freshened world. Stones were man's oldest companions; handling them, the first civilized act. The subconscious commemoration roused by the abrasion on his hands and the pull on his forearm muscles made Conner feel brisk, purged, central; there was a widespread anthropolatry in things of which he was the focus. Above, the sky seemed a mammoth negative which, printed, might prove a Michelangelesque mural; like the long hair of persons fleeing tendrils of vapor unwinding slid sideways across blue patches vivid as paint. Silver rivers lay between clouds.

"Two more such ones," Hook observed, "and you'll have a load."

Resentfully Conner saw this truth. He had been stupid to picture the barrow heaped high with rocks; such a load would break two men's strength. Further it was an error to load the big rocks at all. When the masons came in a few days, he assumed they would want the large rocks that had been already worked. And it was the pebbles that made the look of litter.

"My mistake," he called. "Let's roll the big ones to the wall, and just clean up the rubble. You and I," he said to Gregg, "had better lift this one out again. I'm sorry."

Before he could protest the small wiry man had seized the ends of the stone in his own two hands with an angry sound and carried it to the wall. Showing off. Most of the male inmates had been laboring men. With surprising efficiency the old men rolled the big stones against the wall. This done, they stood facing him, their arms hanging long, and he, an amateur foreman pursing his lips to repress a self-deprecatory smile, demonstrated the next stage by bending and dropping some fieldstones into the wheelbarrow. Gregg, and Tommy Fuller, and a man from the porch, came and consumed with steady clatter the area of loose stuff around and near the wheelbarrow, and the others brought handfuls from further away. Conner, not needed, stood idle, ready to pick up any rocks that missed the target. The distance between the wheelbarrow and the stones to be removed from the grass had increased; the men—several women were also helping now—had taken to tossing them a yard or two. Conner, dully watching the stones accumulate, stones of tints from milk to dung, ranging through lilac, cream, and pencil-gray, many speckled, infrequent ones stratified, did not think to move the wheelbarrow closer. To this extent he was at fault.

Deliberately Gregg flipped one too far. It struck Conner on the left thigh as he stood, his eyes downcast, between the handles. Unhurt and expecting such errors from these feeble people, he automatically bent to retrieve it, and Gregg threw another one, overhand, which stung him on the back, an inch to one side of the spine, thrust up in knobs by his bending. Puzzled, Conner straightened; the abrupt act tipped his brain a second, so that to the off-balance chemicals there the people standing upright at some distance from him seemed weirdly opaque, their presence magical and menacing.

Without his knowledge his white face plainly expressed this moment of fear. His flash of bewildered cowardice jarred loose the last pin restraining Gregg. Half-hidden in the midst of the other old people, Gregg loosed a cry, shaking full of spittle, that stirred them. His wrist whipped where they could see, and a stone dug the grass to Conner's left. Conner turned his back and strode rapidly away, without quite running, and at this retreating target all—Hay and his two friends, Lucas, Tommy Franklin, even Fuller and the women and others who had come freshly to the group —flung small stones, most of them falling short.

One stone of medium size hit Conner on the back of the head, where the skull is thinnest. Stunned and quickly sickened, Conner felt as a revelation dropped from a red heaven the word *unjust*. He wheeled for a moment under the hail of pebbles and glimpsed Hook, the tallest, standing there as if presiding.

Hook had been studying the clouds above the west horizon, where numerous types were superimposed— a bank of indigo making a false sky behind crumbling nimbus suds, bars of high cirrus and faint true sky behind it all—and Gregg's outcry had slowly recalled his mind; stiffly, shifting his gaze but not lowering it, he had his narrow field of vision crossed by a flow of arrowing stones, speeding through the air in swift flocks, and before he considered, he had the thought that here was something glorious. Battles of old had swayed beneath such a canopy of missiles.

It was unjust, but Conner was too much a man of reason to be propelled by an impulse back, blinking, through the onslaught to choke the source. Attempting to assert control, he steadied his gaze on them, even as they threw, while he took a few casual steps backwards; then he decided on disdain, and turned on his heels and kept walking.

As if at the end of a side tunnel Amy Mortis saw in her mind the tiny black figure of Mendelssohn, his heavy head nodding, and, encouraged, she clawed rocks from the ground, flinging one even as she stooped for another; scrabbling and hilariously cawing, she worked her way to the forefront of the pack, and led the second stage, where the ones throwing laughed at the realization of what they were doing. More laughter came from people scattered about the lawn, who at the distance could appreciate the comedy of Conner's pudgy figure stubbornly striding with a vestige of composure beneath the harmless pepper of tiny black objects. Gregg had ceased to throw, and spouted sarcastic obscenities forward.

Buddy came to view the tag end, when Conner was nearly out of their range, and the stones were tossed without seriousness. Amazed as he was, and alarmed for his superior, while his feet raced across the lawn his aloof boy's mind indifferently pictured a newspaper story, himself being interviewed as witness.

"What is this?" Hook asked deliberately, at last conceiving the situation.

"Son of a bitch of a cat-killer, brave bastard run your a.hole off," Gregg called.

Fifteen yards away Conner turned. His cheeks were red, but only at the moment of turning and glimpsing Hook had he moved irrationally. He had known the game would turn within seconds. He stared at the cluster of inmates; two stones fell well before his feet, and then no more.

Buddy stormed right up to them. "You're insane! Do you know what you've done? You'll all go to Fryeton—they'll put you in padded cells!" Fryeton was the insane asylum of the county.

They all seemed to look through him, toward Conner, who softly rubbed his occiput, where the one stone had caught him. "Go away," he said huskily, cleared his throat, and repeated, "Go away." Then, the least expected thing, he stooped and collected a double handful of the stones that had fallen around him, and brought them forward to the wheelbarrow. As he advanced toward them the old people, save Hook, turned and walked away, into the crowd that had gathered. "I know you all," he added to their backs.

Since Conner seemed interested in nothing but gathering the stones, Buddy helped him. No one strayed near them. "How did it start?" Buddy asked.

"I have no idea."

"What are you going to do?"

"Forgive them."

"Forgive them? Just that?"

"All of that. It's a great deal. I'm quite hurt; I had no idea of that much hate."

"But at least you could punish their leader."

"I'm their leader."

Buddy decided this wasn't a joke, for his superior's red hands were trembling so much he had difficulty holding pebbles. Buddy took his master's forbearance as a lesson learned. One of the obscurer lessons, but true to the man, whom Buddy, melodramatically moved, observed passionately: the pores of the wall of his cheek astounding pits, and the curve of his upper lip a marvellous bulge assaulting space. Filled by the forward movement of Buddy's love, the wrinkles at the corner of Conner's eye seemed to mark off significant intervals.

But Conner was feeling that perhaps it was not quite enough, merely to forgive them. The ache on the back of his head dilated and contracted like a living parasitic cap. After depositing the last handful in the wheelbarrow, he came close to Hook, who had held his post and lit another cigar. Conner was convinced that this man had been the cause.

"Mr. Hook," he said, "in your wide experience have you ever seen anything like that madness?"

"Ah," Hook said, "when I was teaching at Furlowe, the children trapped a flying squirrel, and broke its bones with sticks. Bore-dom is a ter-rible force."

"Doesn't there have to be one man to release the force?"

"Now the little fella," Hook said, who had been waiting to make this explanation, "had been sipping alcohol, and had not expected that the cat would be put out of the way." For he had imagined himself, after the others retreated, as staying, as an innocent onlooker, to allay Conner's wrath against Gregg. Hook conceived of himself as a politician and arbiter.

Conner did not know who the "little fella" was. He did not suspect Gregg at all of being the instigator and his case against Hook as a schemer was strengthened. "What made them do it?" he asked.

"Yes, what? Idleness. Idle hands make devil's work," Hook said, suddenly tired and not very interested. The irregularity of the afternoon had worn him. He wished only now to take a stroll, in solitude, around the exterior of the wall.

"Don't they realize what this man has done for them?" Buddy asked, unable to hold his tongue longer, Conner's circumspection again making him impatient.

"I repeat," Hook said, "he was taken aback, and not in his right mind."

"My patience," Conner said, "is not limitless. Any repetition of mass defiance, and there will be measures taken. I promise that. In the meantime I suggest, Mr. Hook, that you yourself stop endangering your own health and the safety of the wooden buildings with cigars and matches. I more than suggest it, I order it."

Not fully understanding, Hook stated, "There is little danger, for a man above ninety. The poor fear no thief."

"He said you're for*bid*den," Buddy said shrilly off the roof of his mouth, and snatched the cigar from Hook's softly posed hand and threw it onto the ground and vengefully stamped on it, though in the deep damp grass the ash continued to smoke.

The expression on Hook's face scarcely changed, and Conner felt, looking up toward the dark woman-ish lips of the disapproving mouth, a wince of grief, as he had when, in connection with some negligible venture, he had balked his own father, a generation ago.

But there was nothing which could be done now which would improve what had been done.

ALIKE FORBIDDEN the dark hours, the old and young came first to the fair, the old for talk and the young for candy. Fred Kegerise, once burgess of Andrews, brought his daughter's son, who was eight. This boy's fresh face ignited anxiety in the heart of his grandfather, who felt the hot flexible hand he held grow slippery and, as they proceeded on their walk, more and more frankly try to pull away. Yet fear of his daughter's disappointment if anything, even skinned knees, happened to the boy kept his grip firm.

As soon as the weather cleared they had set out from their common home in Andrews, Fred's old manse, where his daughter had been reared. When she yearned to marry a boy from Chicago—college had exposed her to all sorts—Fred, enjoying the afternoon of his powerful day, had preyed upon her own timidity and that of his wife, alive then, and between menacing and pathetically wheedling the two women had brought the affair to nothing. Then Annabelle had married a town boy, not the man he would have picked either, but, guilty about the first one, he had let this one go. A dentist, his son-in-law came to live in his great house. Fred had wanted this but not his old sun room turned into an anteroom and his living room partitioned to hold two dental chairs hidden from each other. But by the time this step was taken his day of authority had set. The son-in-law took to sly complaining about supporting the old man and his great house, never letting a fuel bill pass without lament, yet not being man enough to state his thought bluntly: that men who had built for themselves such massive shells must have been crazy with pride. When Fred had built the house solely to let his two women hold their heads as high as any. Esther had needed dignity. His two women's shyness, fitting in the home, had not suited his pretentions in the town. Now Annabelle, her mother gone, sided with her husband against her father. Yet the two of them made no secret, in fact seemed proud, of the grandson's strong resemblance to him. To their shame they were giving the child no religious instruction. His son-in-law had been bold enough to say it did more harm than good in the last analysis.

His grandfather's dry grip enveloping the end of his arm, Mark had walked up Wilson Avenue, where men were digging for the cloverleaf, past the house of the woman who teased, along the wall where fearless bad boys dared run along the top, when a fall would probably break their necks. At all points the poorhouse wall was taller than Mark, a high brown thing to keep the poorhouse people in, though a few sometimes got out and wandered into town and waggled a claw at children coming back to the grade school after lunch. Mark also knew, from older children, that in the field on the other side of the road, way behind, boys from the high school and girls took off their clothes and walked in the car headlights. Mark was in process of subduing the town to memory. Finally there would be no intersection or lot where something had not happened to him, and every crack of pavement would have experienced the tread of his foot in some season of the year. Already he had been to the fair, twice before, and remembered the candy.

Coconut strips, peanut butter eggs, vanilla fudge squares, wax jugs of green syrup you drank then chewed the wax, gingery horehound sticks, penuche in chunks, thick coins of white and pink mint, licorice belts you punched the silhouettes of animals and birds out of, little vegetables of sugar, gum drops in the shape of trademarks, tacky cups of amber, licorice that burned your throat and gave you bad breath, Turkish delight you couldn't touch without spilling powdered sugar, licorice pipes with red dots sprinkled to imitate burning, all loose and unwrapped, jumbled in jars and cardboard boxes.

Mrs. Johnson, the lady who annually managed the extensive candy stand, took pride in the old-fashioned, by-bulk look. Coughdrops that came in boxes she spilled into a tray and sold three for a penny. The boxes cost seven cents each; there was no profit. Most of her candies she ordered from a small firm in Trenton, managed by a man himself old, whose death would be the company's finish.

Under his grandfather's eye Mark with difficulty selected five sorts, which he received in his hands as his guardian paid out a nickel, saying "In town this wouldn't buy the boy a lick of salt."

"With the prices now I wonder that modern people aren't all driven out of their heads," Mrs. Johnson said. "Penny candy used to make a profit of sorts. Now I believe there's a loss. They don't let me keep the accounts any more."

"Not? After you've done this so many years?"

"Yes, these are new times."

Mark ate licorice without great happiness. Their being among the first to arrive embarrassed him; he had the fear that only they would come. He hated worse than even fur in darkness going to empty places. He saw one boy he knew in the second grade at school.

"The people running the country today," Fred Kegerise protested, "are trying to do all God's work instead of their own."

"Well we're all in His hands one way or another," Mrs. Johnson said, resigned.

God: to Mark the word was a vast empty place, yet personified with a mouth and long eyes, always steadily watching him, from the air above the top of a house. "They have whips over there," he said.

"What, son?"

His grandfather bent. The great eroded face, with the inner lips coated brown, frightened him. "I saw a boy I know," he mumbled, limply pointing with his free hand.

"Whips eh?" His grandfather winked at the old woman and in going for his pocket let Mark's other hand drop free; it felt cold as the moisture on it evaporated in the air. "Your mom and dad gave me this to spend on you," he said, and gave an old quarter. "And here's something from your mother's daddy to add to it." He offered, delicately pinched in his two fingers so the circular flash of it was plain, a slick half-dollar, one of the new kind, with President Lowenstein's face molded on it.

Not deaf to the hate in his home, where his parents, at night in bed, whispered bitterly of the old man's self-important ways, and proudly conscious that his grandfather's status there was lower than his own, Mark accepted the large coin sadly, afraid to turn his eyes to his grandfather's lest the old man see through their clear substance into a well of pity. Then he abruptly trotted off to flaunt his money before the acquaintance he had seen.

Hurt that the boy had made no show of gratitude, Fred called after him, "Mind and stay within the wall," and turned to find Mrs. Johnson busy with other customers.

"They want us home by six or I guess they'll call the fire department," he said, regardless.

THOSE PERSONS, a dozen or so, who had stoned Conner had swiftly drifted apart, each seeking separate refuge in the company of the guiltless. Tommy Franklin and the women had their stands to attend to. Lucas went to his wife. The three men Gregg had collected on the porch to share Lucas's rye clung together for some minutes, laughing at their own imitations of Conner's posture and expression at different points of the incident—when the second pebble struck him on the back; when, puzzled, he decided to turn and run; when, after the stone (which both August Hay and another claimed to have thrown) hit his head, he wheeled like a bird with a foot in a trap, his arms spread winglike and his mouth open like he wanted a worm put in it. Hay, with crossed arms and protruding rump, burlesqued the dignified way Conner had stood when the rain of pebbles ceased. "I know you all," another squeaked. Attracted by their muster, Fuller joined them for safety, swelling their laughter. To his perplexity, the brave group dissolved the instant it gained the house; from the vestibule each man took a separate corridor.

They did not know they had been forgiven. And they would have known no more than Buddy knew what Conner meant, "forgiving" them. However, apart from the three with criminal consciences, accustomed as boys to despise and dread the police, the culprits were disposed to forget. Lucas put the case bluntly to his wife: "What can he do? This is no jail or a school. We don't have property he can take from us. He can't take a paddle to us." The exertion of throwing had sobered him and brought his ear back to its customary pitch—a feathery, almost flirtatious, hint of pain. Mrs. Mortis's thoughts were: she had led a common life, no worse than most. Here Conner came tramping in on the heels of Mendelssohn's funeral with a lot of needless improvements, and then he comes down full force on Hook, who from boyhood up had been attended to and ought to be allowed to keep saying his piece now that he was half in the grave. As for herself, anything Conner did to get even was better than the same thing day in and day out; if he killed her tomorrow it would be a blessing.

AS HE had intended Hook circumambulated the wall. Buddy's display put him in mind of high-strung competitive students he had had. In Conner he recognized the type of dutiful good boy who had no defense but forbearance against teasing, and the knowledge that in the end he would succeed. As Hook made his way cautiously over the uneven ground on the other side of the wall, reaching out now and then to touch its damp stones, his angel wrestled with the gloom that overcame him customarily in the late afternoon, when the sun's rays, growing oblique, commenced to turn golden. The grounds were bathed in broad intense sun, a single mammoth shaft down which heaven like a negligent janitor sought to pump into the little re-

mainder of the day sufficient heat to last the night
through. At the edges of two boards laid on the wall
steam curled as if several hidden cigarettes were smok-
ing beneath them. The trees, tousled by the storm,
showed the undersides of some leaves. A flicker cried
kee-yew, yik yik. Birdsong on all sides seemed quick
condensations in the barely less dense matter of
pleased air. Hook's breath worked up and down dry
pipes; the labor of his heart, a faithful servant as old
as himself, he noticed now, and consciously appreciated. The walk of his life—across easy and firm
meadows into the doubtful terrain of stony foothills,
or from another aspect down a long smooth gallery
hung with the portraits of presidents of the United
States—seemed to have its end near. He felt his death—
whom he had called previously that day in jest, the
Gentleman—waiting for him like a woman at the end
of a path; and blinking under the breath of her near
presence he wondered what task she had waiting for
him in the house. He was tired after his day and only
wished to rest. Even listening to her voice would be a
job. Her tasks would have to wait a moment, while he
sat in a chair, and indeed it seemed forever would not
be too long, for him to regain his breath. He could picture no job he would ever be ready again to do. His lips
wrinkled as if a bad taste had wormed into his mouth.
Walking weighed on him. The deep landscape off to
his right called to an appetite he no longer possessed.
The feel of the rocks, which he touched, issued a
protest his spirit for this moment could not rise at.
His legs seemed of a material as insubstantial as that of
the daytime moon, which, shot with blue, had come
prematurely to the northern sky. Hook's farsighted

eyes picked out, jagged and bristling, the houses of Andrews visible from the corner where he paused. Along the town side of the western wall lettered wrappers of candy bars and cigarettes littered the beaten grass. Andrews himself had planted outside the wall a hedge of horse chestnut saplings. Slowly Hook proceeded down the nave of the cathedral that had resulted, whose high roof released spatterings of water coagulate as wax and admitted, in the gaps between shifting leaves, bits of light, cool yet unquiet, like the flames of clustered candles. Between the trunks, the painted houses of the town lunged forward, some not a hundred feet away. Voices led Hook to direct his eyes forward; at the far end, unified by sunshine, townspeople were streaming past, some going in at the southwest gate and others continuing on the long way around. His forebodings lifted at the sight of their gay-making clothes, the round limbs of the children, the young women holding their bodies so upright. It seemed a resurrection of his students, and he sensed that he would never leave them, never be abandoned by this parade.

GREGG had gone like an animal with his kill to the most secret place he could reach rapidly; the open area out back, by the west wing, hemmed in with an irregular outlay of sheds. Buddy had taken the body of the cat away and buried it. Gregg was insanely proud and happy. In all his years he had never dared do such a thing as hurl rocks at the head of another man. His wildness had all been in his mouth, rabid saliva. His entire life, the entire black mass of the great city of Newark, had been funnelled into this one feat. He had shown pastyfaced Conner; he had shown Hay who led laughter against him; he had shown the women he never dared speak to but who had followed him with their stones to add to the pile crushing fat-assed pansyvoiced Conner. He had shown there were rights. Unable to keep his feet still he danced over the plaza of dirt, kicking chips of wood and poking his fist against the deteriorating wooden walls of sheds. Sons of screwed-up f.faced white-faced bitches. Gregg was happy, proud, happy; he had never be-fore dreamed that such intense innocent pleasure ex-isted anywhere in old age. He cried out, so a few patients in the west wing were startled to hear, "Horse's ass!"

HOOK'S "sharper" had arrived from Trenton to pur-chase Mrs. Mortis's quaint and beautiful quilts. This year he wanted to buy them all, he had had such success with the four he had got last year. A slight man with large ears and a red cleft chin that looked as though it had once been burnt, he had discovered that in this age there existed a hungry market for anything—trivets, samplers, whalebone swifts, but-tonhooks, dragware, Staffordshire hens, bleeding knives, mechanical apple parers, ferrotypes, weather-vanes—savouring of an older America. There was a keen subversive need, at least in the cities, for objects that showed the trace of a hand, whether in an ir-regular seam, the crescent cuts of a chisel, or the dents of a forge hammer.

"No," Mrs. Mortis said. "Last year you bought what

I had and there was nothing left for me but to go to bed."

"Missus, I don't ask that you go to bed, only let me purchase what you are offering for sale. Shall we say at half again the asking price?"

"What would you do with them all?"

"Do, Missus? Admire them. Such as this one—look at this lovely little Palladian temple! Where do you find the cloth?"

"It's not easy," she said. "I doubt if next year I'll be able to find any, but I'll be dead then anyway, with luck."

"Twice the asking price," he bid. "Six at twenty dollars, that would be one hundred and twenty dollars."

"What's money to me? You can't give me enough to buy my way out of the poorhouse?" A tilt of her bonnet (itself, he thought, a treasure) strengthened his impression that this was a serious question.

"No . . . no, I suppose not. But tell me, missus, when you work, do you use what they call a 'sewing bird,' a clip in the shape usually of a bird that holds the cloth in its beak? Do you have a wicker sewing basket? Or one of the early Singers, with all that beautiful foliate relief on the pedal? Or pincushions? Pincushions bearing political slogans, or portraits of presidents worked in colored thread, or actual wildflowers?"

"Oh, well," said Mrs. Mortis, who loved to have men in conversation with her, "I haven't looked in Mother's chest in years."

"Butter molds?" he inquired rapidly. "Shoe lasts or bootjacks? Once in a great while, you know, you still find bootjacks in the shape of a beetle or frog. Is the chest painted? With birds dipping their beaks into their throats? That's a very interesting motif. Do you remember your mother using Phoebe lamps? Or pofferje pans? Porringers? Stoneware, creamware? Pewter? Anything, really, I'd be extremely interested."

"Well, I'll maybe look. If you want to give me your address. . . ."

He gave her his card. She said, "So it's like they said, you run a shop and sell what I do for a profit to yourself."

"Profit? Very little. Shop, yes, but as to profit, you'd be the one to make the profit. Modern people don't care for old things; they all want the newest of whatever it is. Gadgets, glass furniture. My shop runs on one part money to three parts love."

"I guess that's so, all the young want new things. There's no reverence, as there used to be. Well, why should there be? What'd we do for them? Here we all sit, outliving our time, a drain on their pockets."

"One hundred dollars, Missus, for the lot. How long has it been since you have had a hundred dollars? And these quilts will be going to someone who appreciates them. This marvellous linen of roses. . . . There must be a dozen colors of thread here."

"Yes, well. You wait a bit and let me have my fun; I spent all day setting this up. Go down there, a man makes little baskets out of peachstones." She half-turned her head, her face completely shielded by the side of the bonnet.

He promised sincerely, "I'll be back shortly. I've enjoyed talking with you, Missus———?" Though she did not answer, he was well pleased with the conversation. Her mother's chest, and she must be eighty herself!

ELIZABETH HEINEMANN sat beside Tommy Franklin at his stand and was saying, "much nicer than I had been led to expect he would be. He was at such a disadvantage, being our prefect yet so much younger; didn't his voice seem boyish?"

Tommy made agreeing sounds. No one had told her of the stoning. She would learn in time. His miniature baskets and animals were selling slowly, at a quarter to adults and a dime to children. Children were better customers. To adults the small objects, at a distance looking like pebbles and when examined seen to be neither toys nor paper-weights nor ornaments, were indistinguishable from those badges and tags given for subscribing to a charity. Having subscribed in previous years they did not wish to do so again and again. Children however recognized the objects as what they were, charms. Children sensed in them the childlike emotion Tommy Franklin had felt making them, in the odd hours, usually at dusk, of the days of the previous year. They were especially pleased by just that place, the hole gingerly widened to make an actual handle free in space, where Franklin in working had himself experienced most satisfaction. Placed in a box or drawer these artifacts would exhale an innocent air like a square of lavender whose scent is never exhausted.

"Are the people coming?" Elizabeth asked.

"Pretty well. The bulk will wait till after supper now that it's rained."

"Perhaps I should go to the house. Does my being here disturb you?"

"No, not at all," he answered. In fact the curious eyes of passersby, shifting from himself to Elizabeth, did affect his tongue, so he was unable to talk fluently enough to keep her mind occupied.

Her lips wavered as she saw herself on the brink of the gulf between here and the security of the house, with no guarantee of soft hands reaching to guide her through the crowds and tables. That she had a need for the bathroom further complicated her worry. For what she wanted in her heart was to remain, in the warm sun, on the edge of this pretty lake of noise.

"Oh the music!" she cried when this broke forth. "I'll stay," she firmly said, as a beautiful girl would whose any decision gives pleasure, because it comes from her.

THE LEADER of the band had gone down and moved his foreign car, placing it among the shipshape American models parked diagonally on the band of untended grass along the outside of the wall, their bumpers jutting into the road. Dazzling distortions of the sun—oblong, parabolic, linear—occurred wherever the curving metal of a car chassis entered a certain angle, burning whitely here regardless of the color of the paint. As he left his car the two cars he was expecting pulled up in tandem. "There's Jack; hey, Jack!" these youngsters called at him, smoke of cigarettes issuing from their windows. "Were you worried, Jack?"

"Hell, it's no worry of mine what happens to you;

go drive in a ditch for all I care," the old leader said back, and the kids howled within their cars, and Jack himself smiled a little, because the kids' familiarity with him was to some extent heartening. As the boys got out, a few old men, the difference muted by the uniforms they all wore, got out also, and had been scrunched in there.

Men of the poorhouse meanwhile had dragged from the barn a great dais of lumber, a table for giants, and, having sledded it over the slippery lawn, inverted it next to the porch, which was the same height. As many of the wicker porch chairs as could be were arranged by the band on this rickety platform, the gray boards giving beneath their black shoes. There were nineteen musicians and the platform accommodated a dozen chairs; the remaining seven, including the parade drum, the tuba, and the cymbals, were seated on a row brought next to the porch rail. The chairs, with their metal tags, remained scrambled ever after. Goaded by their leader, the musicians took positions, each stepping over the bannister in turn, even while women were tacking Old Glory bunting to the front and sides of the platform. Before the hammers subsided they unfolded small music-sheets as tattered and yellowed as the bunting and began to play *March Carillon, Op. 19, No. 2*, by Howard Hanson, and then, their faces wooden as they sought for perfect time, went into *The U.S. Field Artillery*, by Sousa. The music was more than a feature of the fair, it was its atmosphere, a ponderable medium through which the celebrants moved.

Hook, wandering through the crowd with a presiding benificent air, his high head rigidly held and his nostrils slightly flaring, had located Fred Kegerise, with whom he had conversed on occasion before. Like two chieftains meeting upon the ridge that separates their armies, the two men spoke face to face in the exact center of the main path. The mob streamed around them. "Now Cleveland had the mettle," Hook affirmed, repeating himself so the other (whose will to domineer was declared by the sheen of his jaw, remarkably clean-shaven considering that the skin had fallen into an old man's folds, and by a harsh haircut that made him bald as a boy above the ears) would not seize space in which to interrupt, "Cleveland had the mettle. He was no Tilden, to let the carpet-baggers steal the office from him. Not that Tilden failed to do battle out of cowardice, but for the good of the country as he con-ceived it, for the Re-publicans were willing to have another Civil War, now that the profits from the first had drifted through their pockets, to the European wines and fancy women, such as the old Commodore kept. But with all respect for Tilden's for-bearance, a war might have been the lesser evil over Hayes with Vanderbilt managing him, and then the nonentity Garfield and Conkling's man Arthur. Isn't it significant, now, that of the three presidents assassinated, all were Re-publican?" He paused more for breath than for an answer.

"Public office is all changed," Fred Kegerise said. "All these examinations and boards of professors and cities managed by schoolboys they never heard of or asked for—there's not an elective office left, except the highest, and there there's but one party."

"Public office," Hook quoted, "is a Public Trust. Cleveland had that mettle needed to turn the muckrakers out, for a time, though McKinley followed, sinking Spanish ships for show. Why, did you know, in his second term—and the one in between, when the old fella Harrison took over, Cleveland had won the vote but juggling the elector-ate kept him out—in his second term Cleveland had a tumor of the throat, and rather than make the fuss to get the public's sympathy, like that Eisenhower who won on the strength of his de-teriorated heart, Cleveland went upon a boat in the Hudson, and while sitting there on the deck after enjoying a cigar, had a surgeon cut it out, without any anaesthetic but a sip of whiskey, and returned to his duties and it was never known till after his death?"

"A long ways from the boys in power today. Between them and the Russians there's little to choose for my money. Even when I was burgess, so many directives so-called and surveys and poll-sheets came spilling from above, it was like running a department store instead of a town. And that was ten years ago."

"This last decade," Hook claimed, not clear what it meant but feeling the words, momentous and rounded, yearning to be said, "has witnessed the end of the world, if the people would but wake to it."

"They vomited paper on me," Kegerise said with pride, re-envisioning those days when he went to a desk every day, a man responsible for public safety and welfare and permitted, when he chose to inspect street works, to ride the steamroller. "I finally told my councilmen, this isn't a town, it's a wastebasket. Let's go home to our wives and let the state run it itself if it's so anxious."

"I wonder, now, if the lightning Matthew mentioned, as running from east to west, might have referred to the a-tomic bombs."

"Paper diarrhoea," Kegerise insisted, glancing around through the growing crowd for his grandson; the time was nearing, as the shadow of the high house approached the east wall, glinting in the declining sunshine like a rim of pink frosting, when he had promised his daughter to bring the boy and himself home. He had not been deaf to Hook's last saying. But it was a recent rule of his to avoid religious discussion. Though a Christian, a few assaults from his dentist son-in-law had given him a dread of the subject in any form, as a disciplined dog will flatten its ears at the mere sight of a folded newspaper.

The boy Mark was in an ecstasy of suavity. Two years before, when he was six, he had created a neighborhood byword by confiding in his piano teacher's girlish mother, beside him on her porch swing, that he liked to be "where the people are." The dawn of evening, the bright trousers and luminous skirts brushing past him, the weight of silver in his pocket, the smell of crushed grass beneath him, and the net of conversation spread above his head seemed to make good the fantastic promise that someday he would inherit the delights of adulthood. He had purchased a cardboard packet of hollow licorice cigarettes. Tipping two or three outward as in the advertisements, he offered the pack to his friend, who took two and gobbled them roughly, as if they had been any candy. Mark smoked his, placing each nicely between his lips, off-center, and, without using his hands, taking tiny bites, as finely as a rabbit, until the cigarette was down to a butt; the butt he flipped away, sacrificing good licorice to the grown-up world which he felt great enough to reach out and touch, right through the tough intervening mass of future time. He inaugurated each new cigarette by tapping one end, in an inaccurate imitation of a gesture of his father's, on the flat place above his belly; the chest of the white T-shirt had begun to show gray traces. These did not worry him enough to make him doubt the rite. The older brother of his friend came to collect him. He was four grades older, of grown-up height, with a sick skin. He watched Mark show off and laughed and said, "Not on your stomach, good God. On your *thumbnail*." From this instant Mark hated the older boy and did the thing correctly. Stupid because his thumbnail was no bigger around than the cigarette. How to hit it? The mottled face of the older boy hung like a moon where he had stood, after he had gone.

Her working day ending on alternate weeks at five-thirty, Grace the nurse by six was down on the lawn to meet Joe and another couple. They planned to go elsewhere soon, for a dinner, then a night. Grace wore a flowered sheath, reds and browns, and a brief white top, Spanish in inspiration, trimmed in narrow lace, that looked put on backwards: closely set buttons ran down her spine and in front the cloth fell straight and stiffly from her breasts. Joe kept dropping a step behind her, for the flowered cloth tightened across her buttocks, making one plane slanting up into the narrow soft waist. This stretch of cloth, steady and smooth above the vibration of the wrinkles charged with the action of her walking, dizzied him with desire. Beneath the cloth he imagined the triangular plate, hard between pads of fat, where, had she been an animal, her tail would have been attached. Cloth taut over rises—the straight lines of her bolero, boxing her chest—made the cave of Joe's mouth a little dry, knowing it was Grace there.

The band played in the soldierly fashion of gallants who maintain parade formation though between the diminishing numbers new gaps are constantly opened by the enemy's fire. At the place in the arrangement where squadrons of trumpets once chorused, the single high instrument of the jut-jawed man sang out from the unstable platform festooned with antique bunting. When in old days the glockenspiel had been scored for a solo bar, the men simply took their instruments from their lips for these measures and let drums of the imagination supply *Va rum. va rum. va rum de umpity rum de um. va rum. va rum.*

The music dimly penetrated to the cupola. Conner, while in his corner Buddy touch-typed for a third time a budgetary report of great complexity, studied the scene. The grounds were filling up. From this height the people in the crowds appeared to bumble like brainless insects, bumping into one another, taking random hurried courses across the grass. Another successful fair. The deepening blue of the eastern sky was clear, except for a few sweepings of strato-cirrus and for the crooked pale face of the premature moon. He was grateful that the old people would have their entertainment after all. His anxiety on that score was another dead issue.

As he looked the colored lights came on, far-reaching strings of them. It was not quite dark enough for them to make a brilliant effect.

The shock of the incident this afternoon had ebbed enough for him to dare open the door which he had slammed on the fresh memory. A monster of embarrassment, all membrane, sprang out and embraced him. The emotion clung to him in disgusting glutinous webs, as if he were being born and fully conscious. He tried in vain to close the door again on the memory—the little stones flying, the animal cries of the old people, his own necessarily absurd appearance.

The muddled bumping world below would certainly hear of it. In the eyes of the town he would be a fool.

In the eyes of the inmates—their opinion would be less vigorous. There was security for him in their shallowness; their memory was frail, and grasped at ancient things. Present time to them must appear weightless, a thin edge of paper. Further he imagined their judgements of him would be clement; the past seasons had inevitably bred some degree of affection and tolerance. This thought entailed momentarily forgetting who had stoned him. He realized, suddenly and clearly, that the dozen guilty had acted for all; any would have leaped for stones at Hook's signal (which he had not seen). Why? Because, Conner supposed, he was better than they.

At any rate there was nothing to do but persevere in his work. He would not, unlike Mendelssohn, be a poorhouse prefect forever. In another year or two, if his progress here continued to look impressive on paper—the two most important statistics were the yield from the farm and the longevity of the inmates —he would be moved up, perhaps into a State Health Service Council. He expected association with scientists to be pleasanter, more suited to his gifts and to the quality of his dedication. Still, he prized a useful over a pleasant life. Wherever I can serve, he told himself. At the same time his mind ran off a film. He was sitting at a table of dignitaries, not in the center but with becoming modesty at one end. He rose, papers in hand. "My department is pleased to report the possession of evidence which would indicate," he said, and paused, "that the cure for cancer has been found." The turn of his thoughts to medicine recalled, with an ache, the wound on his own skull, and embarrassment surged over him again, with a rushing murmur like that in a seashell. He said aloud, to say something to hide the noise, "A good crowd. It's funny that the town always turns out in strength for such a tame affair."

"The age-old appeal of the freak show," Buddy replied, speaking floridly now that Conner was safely closeted with him. "See the fat lady, who suffers from a thyroid condition; see the alligator man, a victim of psoriasis. See the hermaphrodite, deified in ancient Greece."

"Do they still have those? Freak shows? Jesus as a kid they used to give me the holy horrors."

"I must confess I've never been to one in person. Weren't they attached to circuses?"

"You're too young," Conner said. "You didn't miss a thing."

He was tempted, in his need for consolation, to let his tongue run on before this boy, but sensed that silence now was in order. There was a danger of over-encouraging fondness. Buddy's love, or that of any one soul, was not to Conner's purpose.

Cars were parked the full length of the wall; more came slowly up the road. Buddy's white hands resumed their quick tapping. On the grounds below, the broad shadow of the house muted distinctions; tables, heads, cartons, white arms, flashes of cloth and patches of grass seemed cells of one living conglomerate, through whose sprawling body veins of traffic with effort circulated: a beast more monstrous than any he had told Hook of. For the third time a wave of embarrassment swept over him—he had been mocked—but within he stubbornly retained, like the spark of life in the shattered cat, the conviction that he was the hope of the world.

HEART had gone out of these people; health was the principal thing about the faces of the Americans that came crowding through the broken wall to the poorhouse fair. They were just people, members of the race of white animals that had cast its herds over the land of six continents. Highly neural, brachycephalic, uniquely able to oppose their thumbs to the four other digits, they bred within elegant settlements, and both burned and interred their dead. History had passed on beyond them. They remembered its moment and came to the fair to be freshened in the recollection of an older America, the America of Dan Patch and of Senator Beveridge exhorting the Anglo-Saxons to march across the Pacific and save the beautiful weak-minded islands there, an America of stained-glass lampshades, hardshell evangelists, Flag Days, ice men, plug tobacco, China trade, oval windows mark-

ing on the exterior of a house a stair landing within,
pungent nostrums for catarrhal complaints, opportun-
ism, churchgoing, and well-worded orations in the
glare of a cemetery on summer days. The London
Pacts with the Eurasian Soviet had been new in the
experience of America, who had never fought a war
that was not a holy war, and never lost one once begun. There was to be no war; we were to be allowed
to decay of ourselves. And the population soared like
diffident India's, and the economy swelled, and iron
became increasingly dilute, and houses more nig-
gardly built, and everywhere was sufferance, good
sense, wealth, irreligion, and peace. The nation became one of pleasure-seekers; the people continued
to live as cells of a body do in the coffin, for the
conception "America" had died in their skulls. "Why,
in Nero's day," Hook was saying in their midst, "they
had peace a-plenty. And such an odor was e-mitted
his name even today is recalled as easily as that of
Lincoln. Now, the officials express surprise that
so many of the high-schoolers have taken to homosexu-
ality. Per-version is the most natural thing in the
world, once pleasure is conceived of as something for
more than evening hours."

The man—middle-aged, sunburned—he was addressing nodded appreciatively; he had come to hear
such talk as this. Every sentiment of Hook's was as
precious to him as a piece of creamware or a sewing
bird to the antique dealer from Trenton. "You don't
mean," the man protested, "your God don't want us
to have a happy minute."

"Ah, yes,"—Hook lifted a brown forefinger to

within half an inch of his trimmed mustache— "but minutes given as a present, while the hands are busy with serious matters."

"You can't think we ought to be at war all the time. I fought in a war, you know."

"There is a war we can wage without blood. Now Nero murdered his mother as the logical out-come of his philosophy. What surprises me in this day and age is that everyone doesn't do the same. Make no mistake. There is little store of virtue left."

Thus pronouncing, Hook had a very clear inner apprehension of what virtue was: An austerity of the hunt, a manliness from which comes all life, so that it can be written that the woman takes her life from the man. As the Indian once served the elusive deer he hunted, men once served invisible goals, and grew hard in such service and pursuit, and lent their society an indispensable temper. Impotent to provide this temper, this salt, men would sink lower than women, as indeed they had. Women are the heroes of dead lands.

Hook felt the burden of his intuition as unique within him; but perhaps, less heavily, it existed in many of the hearts around him. Andrews was a small town, a backwater: most of its inhabitants were only a few generations removed from farm owners. They passed among the handmade quilts, loose candies, pyramids of sweet corn, and the sage misshapen faces of the inmates as in certain industrial processes a liquid to be purified passes, bubbling, through a bed of mineral fragments.

"I said not to do that."

"Well, we don't know. We hope but we don't know for sure."

"So I asked him why, because I wondered, and he wouldn't tell me."

"*Don't.*"

"You're probably the last person on the street to know, so I see no harm in telling you what's common knowledge anyway."

"My poor sicklies," Grace said. "Up there all alone."

"He came home pale as a sheet and went upstairs to wash his face by himself, which he never does, and after the longest time told me about this man he had met."

"You know how when she comes home at night she crosses the Leonards' back yard to get into her own. I guess she doesn't dare in her condition to walk the full way around."

"You want to really? *I'd* like to, but I don't see why any of you . . . Joe? All right?"

"Didn't you hear me? I said *don't do that.*"

"Yes, you have to have hope."

"I love you all."

"The principal says he has an idea who the man was. Respectable, is all he'd say. You'd think we'd have a right to know, wouldn't you?"

"So Leonard leans from the window and shouts, so you could hear it six houses down, Get off my flowers, you—well if he said it I suppose I must—whore. Get off my flowers, you whore."

"Must Daddy spank you?"

They felt the poorhouse would always be there,

exempt from time. That some residents died, and others came, did not occur to them; a few believed that the name of the prefect was still Mendelssohn. In a sense the poorhouse would indeed outlast their homes. The old continue to be old-fashioned, though their youths were modern. We grow backward, aging into our father's opinions and even into those of our grandfathers.

WHILE the festivities in front were flattened in the plane of shadow, the west wing received the benefit of the declining sun, which hung behind the smoked glass of the lower atmosphere, orange, oblate, and distended. More color than light, it was bearable to look at. Eyes whose pupils like its image had enlarged in growing darkness studied without squinting this blank medallion. Angelo had gone home. Except for the echo of band music the room was quiet. All the energy used for moans and talk was consumed in the reception, by tiny discs of sensitive plate embedded in faces in turn embedded in pillows, of the horizontal rays of the daily omen. Orange bars streamed parallel to the beds; from the peaks on the sheets conic shadows fell upward, toward heads and shoulders, slashing linen which was, in the contrast, faint green-blue. Sunset in the summer was framed between two horsechestnut trees; in winter one tree obscured it, fretting its unpredictable colors with a system of twigs that never changed. Tonight, a bank of gray, like washed slate upon which the schoolchild's sun had been pasted, sloped upward into purple, and changed to soft cloth, undulating in long even folds as if crimped for display. At the horizon stood the thunderheads of the storm that had passed. Diminished by distance and pierced by light, they seemed transparent. The air was unmarked except by their blue outlines, dividing a gray that was cool from one within that was (heightened in the sky's superior scale of luminiscence) the same dull lilac Hook had observed shining through the ears of the rabbit on the grass beyond the wall.

Grace and her three companions entered the room softly. For all of them—even Grace, whose pity, foreknowing its object, was most moved—it was something of a prank. Ascending the stairs they had talked in whispers. "Night Nurse look in yet, Mrs. Dice?"

"Why Grace," this woman murmured, whose kidneys would never let her rest. "Aren't you off?"

"Yes, honey. See how I'm dressed." She lifted her round arms and moved backward, so it could be seen that beneath the white bolero jacket a street dress flowered.

"Oh. Pretty."

"These are my friends. We've come to see how you're enjoying the fair."

Mrs. Dice turned her head and said to Joe, "She's an angel to us. We wouldn't last without her." Her eyes fastened on the paper bags in his hands.

"We've brought some things they're selling," Grace explained. "Which would you like, Mrs. Dice? Apples or candy?"

"Oh, dear. I can't refuse candy." She took a piece of chocolate and, since Joe did not immediately snatch the bag from under her hovering hand, another. "No one but you would have thought of us, Grace," she said, with an expression of pathetic daughterly gratitude slowed and made solid by complacence, to which Grace's too-fleeting and tentative expression of maternal serenity exactly corresponded. For Grace, here in her love dress, felt queer, whereas Mrs. Dice lay on a bed drenched with her existence and inseparable from it, and was more hostess than guest.

Aware, through the eyes of the immobile patients, of their health's splendor, the young people drifted, with a patter of shoes, through the beams of red sunshine that scored the room like a sheet of music-paper. Grace did not introduce her friends by name. Made timid by the thought that their presence might be a breach of regulations, she communicated stealth to the expedition. To some bewildered eyes the rays of sunshine seemed visible through these visitant bodies, a bar persisting now through a waist, now a set of shoulders.

The girl who was not Grace took an apple for herself and bit into it sharply; the moisture of her lips glistened around the white crescent she had opened in the skin. She was rapidly growing at ease in this ward, which upon her entering it had given her a choking feeling, shocked as she was by the absence of oranges and flowers. She moved away from the group, visiting beds independently, asking, "How are you feeling? Don't you see lovely sunsets here? Wouldn't you like your pillow plumped? Let me." As the young people moved from bed to bed, emptying their paper bags, hilarity swelled in the ward. Old people leaned their heads toward one another and compared candies. As a joke Grace left a licorice pipe on Angelo's desk. The tide of conversation, dry laughter of surprise, exclamations—"Wasn't that charitable?" "Gum drops and I have no teeth." "Who would have thought?" "Winesap, this one." "When she straightened my pillow I thought I'd scream with the pain." "Such a pert blouse." "Did you notice how Grace's boy kept his eyes on her behind?"—continued in the great room (Mrs. Andrews' foolish ballroom) for minutes after the young people had left, then gradually subsided into silence before the new and tragic spectacle the wide windows were offering.

The disc of the sun was no longer seen. Opaque air had descended to the horizon, hills beyond the housetops of the town. On one side, the northern, a slab of blue-black, the mantle of purple altered, reared upward; on the other, inky rivers tinged with pink fled in one diagonal direction. Between these two masses glowed a long throat, a gap flooded with a lucent yellow whiter than gold, that seemed to mark the place where, trailing blue clouds, a sublime creature had plunged to death. The titanic yellow furrow dimmed into blue as it approached the zenith, now capped by night, and was rounded like a comet head nearest the horizon, where the color was most intense, the color of an unnatural element, transuranic, created atom by atom in the scientist's laboratory, at inestimable expense. Off to the south the rivulets of dark vapor left in the wake of the catastrophe broadened into horizontals pale by contrast to the deepening sky behind them. Upon the terraces of these ranged clouds blackish embryos of cumulus stood on their tails like sea horses or centaurs performing. As the patients watched, the golden chasm shaded, through faint turquoise, into blue, and clouds propelled by evening winds trespassed its margins.

WEARY of his wife's chatter—always about Joan, Joan who was always on the move, never in one place a week, who wished this parakeet on them, always wishing things on them yet not writing two letters a year, her husband not steady, always on the move, why can't they have a nice home like we gave her? why can't they make roots?: all this when Martha should know that the world had changed and Joan was moving with it—Lucas left the porch and went out back to see the hogs. In crossing the open space between the outbuildings he stepped on the spot where, throughout the storm, the cat's body had lain. Lucas rested his forearms on the rough breadth of the top rail. His ear hurt slightly. Within the pen the swine drifted in small families, sucking and snorting; rippling lips slapped wet teeth and exhalations poured whistling through contracted nostrils. One huge Hampshire hog, a king, groaned rhapsodically as he staggered up from a pit of mud. Lucas minded the stench of the pen no more than the smells of his own body. Between his teeth he crooned, "Sooey. Sooey. Sow sow sow." Dignified by dark into silver zeppelins, the sleepy swine drifted toward him, their sharp feet sucked by the soft ground, their voices raised to a pitch of expectation. Embarrassed at the misunderstanding—had had nothing to give them; morning was their time—Lucas said, "Look at your trough. Half-full." A few carrots and grapefruit rinds remained in the trough; the pigs disdained these.

The lights in the west wing came on. Night Nurse had entered. The squares of artificial light cast this distance touched with yellow the notched ears, made a brown eye shine, caught the innocent faces in something of their pinkness, and turned the shell of half a lime vivid green. As at the approach of day the pigs squealed gaily; the tits of a great sow stood out erect. The Hampshire hog collapsed on his side with a brilliant peal, and a single tide of fat swung across his body. Then Night Nurse cut back the electricity, letting a few bulbs guide her. As the general body of pigs withdrew into the darker reaches of the pen, a few flung back, across their haunches, looks of distrust at the silhouette of the spy leaning on the fence. One baby, paralyzed on rigid legs, abruptly rooted at the lime rind, and wheeled and fled, crying.

What could Conner do to them? A man with a family was always more vulnerable than one who had none. It had been he who had brought the bottle of rye onto the property. Conner had said, *I know you all.* Buddy would uncover everything. He sensed that Buddy hated him, because he did not treat Conner as a god but as a human and got him dirty that way. Tomorrow he had better see Conner in his office. Were anything to happen the shock would crumple Martha's legs. The bottle, was it still on the porch? Better find it, throw it on the trash.

By an unexpected tension beneath his eyes he learned that he was smiling. He had remembered a domestic incident of thirty years ago. Joan was just two. Poor Eddy was a new baby. Martha had been lying upstairs, trying for an afternoon nap, and Joan, wakened from hers, came downstairs to her father. Lucas from where he sat on the sofa had heard Joan and Martha talking. The child's forehead was bumpy with a frown. "Don't," he had said, reaching out to smooth the skin.

"Whez ahm?"

"Where's what? Did you have a good nap?"

"Whez *ahm?*" Her eyes widened. "In, in *bakket*, with boko bottle."

"Martha," he had shouted, "what is she saying?"

There had been no reply but the sound of Martha's laughter.

"Martha, what did you tell Joan?"

Her laughter, louder, tumbled down the stairs. The child had gone into the kitchen, and Lucas found her at the wastebasket, taking out boxes and scraps. "Burn bottles," she explained earnestly, knowing this was naughty. "Whez mommy *ahm?*"

This much he understood: a few days before, Martha had let the water boil away under two bottles she was sterilizing for Eddy, and the sight of these cracked and blackened bottles had worried Joan considerably. "The bottles aren't there any more," he told her.

Then Martha came down, small-eyed from her nap and laughing, and hugged the child and showed her her left arm and said, "Here's Mommy's arm. See: two arms. You can't take an arm off and put it in the wastebasket. It was Mommy's joke. It's all right, sweet. Oh, sweetie. Little girl." She explained to Lucas that Joan had crawled up on the bed while she was napping on her side, and had asked where was the other arm. Yielding in her drowsy state to a silly impulse, she had answered that Mommy had grown tired of her arm, it was no good, and she had thrown it away, with the burnt bottles.

They laughed together and consoled with embraces the puzzled girl, who for the next days continued to poke in the wastebasket. It had moved them close to tears to discover that the child, whose vocabulary and cunning daily fattened, could still be deceived so outrageously, her trust in her parents so far exceeding her knowledge of things.

"WHORE? she says. Is that what I am? So that's what you call me? And calm as you please she pulls out every one of his tulips and gladiola, and tosses them into his birdbath. This about two a.m. in the morning, mind you."

"Come on, Maryann. Why not? Just tell me why not."

"Isn't she beautiful? I think the blind are always so calm, as if, you know, they see things we don't."

"No now," Hook said, "the people nowadays have it so good, they are unable to con-ceive of a better place awaiting them."

"Yes, the blue of her eyes."

"Well, I slept through everything, but Jack says it was Leonard's bellow woke him up. And nobody sleeps sounder than Jack, usually; I'm the one who's awake at the drop of a pin, usually."

"Anybody else would, if they liked a person. Come *on*. We promise nobody'll touch you."

"I suppose," Kegerise admitted, "I should be heading home myself. I told them I'd have the boy home by six."

"We promise on a stack of telephone directories nobody'll touch you."

"Yes, as innocent as a baby's. Do you suppose she really is? She moves them just like anybody else."

"It was awfully sweet of you all. I really feel like having a good time now."

"The time is ap-proaching when us old fellas should be climbing the wooden hill. Rafe Beam, my father's hired man, used to recite,

> 'Late in bed,
> Soon dead.
> Up by dawn,
> Never gone.'"

A young couple was interested in one of Mrs. Mortis's quilts. The boy was saying, "No ma'am, I don't want to let you do that. Your price is fair, it's just that, Honest to God, we don't have the M-O-N-E-Y."

The girl said, "Here's a patch exactly like the wallpaper we want for the living room."

"Honey, we can't ask the lady to let us pay a dollar a week or anything like that."

"Jack says he heard Leonard shout he was calling the police. You know how you can hear a pin drop on that street since all the lovely elms died. Jack said she said, and I couldn't repeat the exact words, that he could take the police and push them up his pants and furthermore she hopes they do come, because what he said to her was slander. Which I suppose is true. She never takes money."

"All we want to do is *see*. Dotty's agreed."

"I have *not*."

"What would it hurt? Just tell me one thing it would hurt."

"When she bit that apple I thought I'd crawl under a bed."

"Look how she touches the sleeve of the man. They must be in love."

"Isn't *he* a horror though? What *are* those things he's selling?"

"I guess we *do* have seven dollars. But—"

"We'll let you see *us*."

Conner from above wished they would disperse; the quicker they dispersed, the less chance there was of the story of today's incident spreading among them. Thinking of the incident made his stomach tremble with nervousness. Buddy came over and stood beside him, placing a hand on Conner's shoulder, then dropping it to his waist. Conner pulled away, amazed and annoyed. Buddy flushed, pardoned himself, and went downstairs, leaving the office divided between Conner and the unused piano.

"Now I think I *will* spank you."

"But where should we go? *Not* Lorry's again. Anything but Lorry's."

"How could it hurt you? What are you ashamed of? Huh? What are you ashamed of?"

"He went around in his pajamas to their front porch, and the only thing there of course was their rubber welcome mat, so he tried to tear it with his bare hands and couldn't. He actually had the presence of mind, while she had let herself into her half by the kitchen door and was weeping and waking up her girl—the husband of course was off at work; his working nights is ninety-nine per cent of her trouble if you ask me—Leonard actually had the coolness to go back into his house, get his gardening shears, and cut the rubber welcome mat into tiny bits while she's in her front parlor shouting at him through the window. She was scared to come out and I don't blame her, he's so big."

"Oh, I'm too old for shopkeeper's hours," Mrs. Mortis said aloud to herself. "Where's that chair I begged?"

"What do you mean, not nice? If your own body's not nice, what is? Why not shoot yourself if you don't want a body?"

"Ken boy! I missed you at Lions. Kay here? I wanted to ask her how did *she* enjoy Florida? I know *you* enjoyed it."

"Your body's yours, isn't it? It's not your mother's or anybody's."

Buddy had found someone he knew, a young man who worked in Town Hall, where Buddy sometimes went on business. To him and his companions he said immediately, "Do any of you know what the hell happened here this afternoon? The ancients in residence in this pleasure-palace seized rocks the size of suckling pigs and brained their shepherd, the reverend Mr. Conner. Seriously."

"I think living in a double home like that, with just the partition between families, must build up tensions. I'm so thankful we have grass on all four sides of us, even if it's not much as yards go."

"Indeed it is not wise, to dis-obey one's daughter. The warmer the love, the harder the tem-per bites."

Hook made these words his farewell to Kegerise, who, certain of being more than an hour late, was beginning to perspire unhealthily. His eye caught his grandson, himself tired and queasy, coming to be taken home. Hook went onto the porch, at the end farthest from the band, which was taking a rest, and lit a cigar, his day's last. Conner's childish prohibition had quite faded from his mind. His mind vaulted far over it. The level farm land beyond the merrymakers might well have been, in the darkness, water, steadily flowing beneath its unbroken black skin. Near at hand Mrs. Johnson waited behind her display of candies. Hook remembered an incident of twenty years before, when he had been an old man, as now. He had retired from schoolteaching and lived with the family of his daughter, then alive, in a rural house several miles outside of the town beside the Delaware. They rented the land to a combine. At the bend of a nearby highway Harry Petree operated a modest store, a shack of two rooms. In one there was a wood stove and the papers of several Sundays ago; in the other a case of candy, and shelves of cigarettes, cigars, lighter fluid, scotch tape, ballpoint pens, and other oddments for which there was small demand. In the summer months Harry kept a tank of soft-drink; the old flavors, lime, sarsaparilla, birch. Outside two gasoline pumps stood, the outmoded bubble-head style. Because the shack was at a bend of the road, the high-powered cars came upon it too late to brake, and indeed they may have thought, from the look of the place, that it was deserted. Whatever the cause, few stopped. Perhaps Harry did three or four dollars worth of business a day, on the cigars and candy occasionally purchased by the old men—Hook alone still living—who loitered out the afternoons in the room with the wood stove. Harry was an uncouth, almost savage man, very short in stature, never without a great wad of tobacco plug in his mouth, a stain dribbling from the corner of his gray lips. He spoke in a growl, garbled by the piece of plug, which it took a considerable period of acquaintance to understand. He and his sister owned the land; she did housework around the neighborhood, and he had a small pension, as a veteran of the first world war. They lived in their father's sandstone house, by the light of kerosene, well back from the road. With their truck garden, they survived, but never had the money for improvements, at the house or at the store. In the seven years Hook had his acquaintance, Harry grew blacker in the face, and growled more and more obscurely. The children of the countryside around were frightened of him, and seldom came into the dark shack, where the candies waited beneath the curved case. One day in the spring, the gasoline company, of its own accord, changed the two rusted pumps to squat, square, red, new pumps, visible for a mile, and hung a new sign on the pole. That week a young man in an expensive car stopped and had Harry fill up the tank. It was a powerful car, with a big tank, and it came to sixteen gallons and over four dollars. Holding a creased twenty-dollar bill between his fingers, the young man asked Harry if he would fetch him a pack of cigarettes, and while Harry was within pulled away and disappeared down the road. Harry lingered at the store a few more days, his eyes no darker than the skin around them and the juice spilling unrestrainedly from his lips, telling the story to whoever would listen. Then the store was shut, which had stayed open often as late as ten, while the wags loitering there completed their conversations. The screen door was padlocked and Harry never came down from the sandstone house. In a short while, nursed by his sister, he died, of liver and heart. Then all the neighbors, who had never patronized the store except for odd gallons of gasoline to get them into town, sent fifteen-dollar bouquets to the funeral, and the recollected sting of those fragrant banked blooms, or perhaps it was the smoke of his cigar, caused Hook's eyes to water behind their shields of glass.

At the time his daughter had scolded him, "Yes, now you can grieve; but did you ever buy ten pennies worth from the old man, instead of sitting there rollicking at all hours, when he wanted to be in bed?" He had explained, he had never thought, and how much money did he have to spend? But now, as he stood there on the porch, it seemed that in the whole vast tract of his life this was the one offense, the one sin against God sharp enough to make a film of regret mount in his eyes.

He opened his mouth idly, as if again to offer his explanation to his daughter.

He cast his mind ahead, to the trip up the stairs, the "wooden hill," and the hard chair and firm bed, and the Bible, its spine in shreds, from which he would read a chapter of the Gospels, those springs of no certain bottom, which you never find dry. But these

doings seemed to lie far distant in the future, more distant even than the backward horizon of his life, and for
the present his old man's thin tears, magnified by his
spectacles' strong lenses, sank, one great transparent
membrane, over the entire gay scene.

"Because your father and I *said* so."

"Well, come with us and watch Dotty do it. You
can't mind that."

"Then the good man simply states, 'I forgive
them.' And the doddering assassins disappear into the
crowd. And that's the high tone of the management
we have down here."

"Then in fifteen minutes the police car was going
up the street. The green light on top was winking
but the siren wasn't blowing, not at two a.m. From
my window I just saw that it was Benny Young driving, sober for one night of the week. The way he
carries on at the fire hall I don't know what he dared
tell them, but there wasn't any more noise from that
end of the street, and the next morning her daughter
walked past on the way to school, her books in her
arms, as normal as you please. She's such a nice girl.
You can't get her to say a word against her mother."

"I won't if Maryann won't. I won't anyway."

"You can see the headlines," Buddy said, spacing
the bars with his fingers in the air,

"POOR PELT PREFECT
CONNER STONED
ON DAY OF FAIR."

"The first day we made Raleigh, and the next we
really pushed ourselves and stopped just this side of
Jacksonville, at a very fine motel, to give ourselves

leeway next day, so we could get there in time for a swim before supper. Man that sea felt like a million dollars."

"Oh, we're not worried yet."

"Tell him I asked after him."

"I told him: brother, you're psychological."

"Now see what you've done, Maryann. Proud of yourself? I bet you are. I'm going to tell everybody you're frigid."

"Have you heard about any trouble they had with the inmates this afternoon? I guess they didn't want to go on with the fair."

"Her eye was swollen so you couldn't see the lashes."

"Well," Mrs. Mortis said to the dealer from Trenton, "I sold one by giving it away. You can have the rest I guess." She was lapsed into her chair, her little head, in its stiff bonnet, sunk on her goiter.

"This is wonderful news, missus. Look, I bought from your friend down the line some of these trinkets." He showed a handful of Tommy Franklin's carved peachpits. "In my profession, you never know what people will buy. Now let us see. I said a hundred dollars for six, so for five that would be, oh, eighty-five dollars."

"Whatever is fair. These are my last. I won't do any more."

"It kills me to hear you say that. Suppose I sent you cloth?"

"Send it care of my casket."

Upstairs Conner was rereading, for the tenth time, the letter that had preyed on him since morning. It

was a kind of sickness, to run his eye through it again
and again:

Stephen Conner—
Who do you think you are a Big shot? Yr duty is
to help not hinder these old people on there way to
there final Reward. I myself have heard bitter com-
plant from these old people when they come into
town where I live. They call you Pieface you and
that moran Buddy. The nature of there complants I
will disclose latter, and will write the U.S. gov.ment
depending. Things have not gone so far these old
people have no rights no pale peenynotchin basterd
can take away.

A "Town's person"

A woman, certainly. Conner remembered from
textbook cases the resources of obscenity to be found
in spinsters. The handwriting was painfully, jerkily
formed, on five and dime notepaper with the kind of
blue ballpoint Conner associated with post offices.
The capitals had all the superstructure of the orthodox Spenserian hand that had been taught in public
schools forty years ago. Each *r* was an anvil. The two
abbreviations hinted at some acquaintance with making out bills and invoices. The Townsperson had become very real to him, with her swinging strings of
black beads and wideset, flat, dim, hysteric eyes, the
eyes of Christian Science. Like his old music teacher,
when he lived in Wilmington. He moved to the piano, lifted the varnished lid, and beat out several
harsh chords in her memory. This chased the sad
phantom. He was grateful that tomorrow would be
a normal day. Ever since he could remember, he hated
holidays.

"Before we got there we wondered if the people at
this hotel wouldn't, you know, act above us. From

what we were paying it seemed they might. But not at all, they were common as dirt—real people. Kay had a wonderful time. This one woman from St. Louis and she struck up a real friendship. While me and her husband—he sold parts to the knitting industry and cleared over twenty thousand a year, but he was humble, a hell of a good egg—while we were down on the beach Kay and the wife sat on the porch yakkity yakkity yak. Kay didn't go into the sun six times all the time we were down there. Her skin stayed just as white—I said to her, here we are, paying thirty dollars a day for this sunshine, and you sit up there yakking away all day. But then what the hell, on a vacation you should do what you want, is the way I look at it. Her skin just as white as that moon up there."

"At first they thought it was an allergy but now they've decided it's an infection. The doctor said, penicillin, and I told him, you don't know my daughter. She will *not* take medicine. He said, she'll take this and want more. You know what it was?"

"Ken, this is interesting. I'm as happy you had a good time as if I had it myself. You convinced me the people that say Wildwood is just as good are full of crap. Say, speaking of nothing, I glanced in at your house when you were off, and it looks to me that with a fresh coat *now*, it would do you for five more years."

"Banana penicillin!"

"Maryann," the boy whispered to the girl he wanted to walk naked in front of his headlights, "I love you, can't you understand? Look." He took out his switchknife and holding the blade at an angle pressed it deeply into the white of his forearm, so deeply that in the crook of the arrow-shaped purple bruise one drop of dark blood appeared.

"Am I impressed," Dotty said.

"I'll do more if you don't," he said to Maryann, ignoring Dotty, who was safe, "deeper this time." He began.

Maryann said, "You dope; don't."

He said urgently in her ear, "I love you that much, is what I'm trying to say. I'd cut off an arm to prove it. I'd eat s. for you; I mean it: *anything*. I love you, love love love love *you*, *e*verything about you; can't I see what I love? I'd do anything for *you*."

"Fred, I know you're sincere, and you wouldn't tell me just to drum up business, but to be frank, after this vacation I'm strapped for spare cash. You know how I am; if I can't pay on the nail, I don't buy. That's the way I've operated, and it's a method that's stood by me."

"Now we're going home and you're going to get a spanking."

"It doesn't surprise me. You need to have an older man in a drab job like this. The state just loves these younger men, but you sometimes need a man with a look of authority. Nothing ever happened I'm sure when that one was here who was in the tavern so often. With the big head."

Indeed Mrs. Mortis was thinking, as she walked across the grass, her apron pockets full of dollar bills, *Not like in Mendelssohn's day* . . .

Mendelssohn, Mendelssohn in his beautiful knobbed casket, a carnation in his lapel, legs pillowed in satin, can we believe that he will never rise? Grass returns.

Perfectly preserved his blind lids stretch above the crumbled smile. The skin that life has fled is calm as marble. Can we believe, who have seen his vital nostrils flare expressively, revealing in lifting the flaming septum, the secret wall red with pride within, that there is no resurrection? That bright bit of flesh; where would such a thing have gone?

"Well," Maryann said, "let's get away from here anyway. Everybody's going home." The four children went to the one boy's car, and while he anxiously coaxed the old motor—the glow from the dash catching the orange arcs of the girl's clipped, tossed hairdo and glazing the flat of her cheeks—the radio warmed and sang:

> "Bajo de la peña nace
> la rosa que no quema el aire."

In the silence of the band, which had stopped to smoke and wipe the instruments, the snatch of tune drifted over the wall into the crowd.

It was not true that everyone was going home. It was not yet eight o'clock; the adults, disposed in groups of three and four, were just warming to each other. Only a few children, the offspring of irresponsible homes, raced between their legs and wrestled on the trampled grass, which was starting to exhale dampness as the dew set in. The pyramids of sweet corn were diminished to a few bruised ears. The women on hot dogs wondered if they should send to the kitchen for another pack; the buying seemed to be over. Tommy Franklin had led Elizabeth Heinemann to the porch. Under the colored lights Mrs. Johnson scolded two giggling boys who had attempted, under cover of a penny purchase, to steal some cough drops. They constantly edged one behind the other, like a deck of two cards shuffling itself.

"He was absolutely right. She loved it. I gave myself a spoonful, and it was delicious. It *was*. The druggist said you can get it in peach and cherry and orange flavors too."

"The thing is this, Ken. Your paint now is in good shape. Another summer of this heat and it will start to flake. Now it would be to my advantage, if I was solely concerned in making work for myself, to let you let it go until it really needed it, then the scraping down would add, say, three hundred to your bill. Slap it on *now*, and the whole house could be done for, well, if you want an estimate I'll be glad to come over."

"I'll talk it over with Kay."

"At first it seemed to make it go up more. Well, John said, another ten dollars down the drain, and poor Popeye's worse than ever. When she had this condition, he called her Popeye. I said, wait a minute. You can't go around saying all doctors are crooks. You have to believe somebody."

"I'll say this. A big outfit would charge you fourteen hundred for one coat. That's a fair-sized house you have there, and all that trim is what makes a job long. We used to figure eighty dollars for a twelve-pane window. But if you were, and I'm just saying this so when you talk it over with Kay you will have something concrete to go on, if you were to let me do it between now and Labor day, when I still have my summer boys, I'd say, oh—" He squinted.

"The next day a little splinter of blue showed."

"Oh, eleven fifty, at a very rough guess. Without the grape arbor."

"Hey wait for me."

"Kay loves that place, I can tell you that much. On the way back, did I mention it, past Baltimore, I was doing, hell, I was doing eighty, and she steps on my foot and floors the accelerator and keeps it there. Don't poke, she says, I want to get home. I didn't think going eighty miles an hour was poking, but I said, You're the doctor. We'll die happy."

"Now it's just a little droopy, but *he* says we don't know what caused it, and what's to prevent it from coming back and us being in hock to the doctors for the rest of our life? I told him, Relax. Have a little faith."

"Wa-it, for Chrissake!"

"That's just like the Kay I knew: the original live wire. When I knew her at school, Ken, there wasn't exactly grass growing under her feet. She's every inch a woman, as of course you'd know."

"I kind of hope, really, it doesn't clear up for another few days, so I can try the peach flavor."

"I'll level with you Fred. I don't think I can swing it after this wonderful vacation. The house looks good to me."

"Don't laugh. The banana was really yummy; I pity you, having such healthy brats."

"Hey wai-it *up.*"

The north horizon glowed at the place where, deep in a field behind a rise, the two girls stiffly basked in the headlights, wondering what emotion they should feel, and what eyes might be in the trees. The boys, staring, were hidden beyond the opaque windshield, the girls' clothes lying neatly in their laps. Above, the stars were not specks but needles of light suspended point downward in a black depth of stiff jelly. The band resumed its sheaf of Sousa with *American Patrol*, played *dolce*, then *forte*. The effect created was that of a band coming toward you from far down the street. A disturbed sparrow dipped under the string of burning colored bulbs, taking crimson on its back for an instant. The people who had come to the fair talked more slowly, tending toward affectionate gossip about the past they had in common as citizens of the town, and about roads and schools and old houses sold. Coarsened hands of still handsome women nervously tucked back stray strands of hair; young mothers pouted under the weight of sleeping babies. Above them in the cupola Conner worked unseen, checking Buddy's typed reports. Except for Gregg and a few weary biddies keeping their stands going, the old people had vanished from this crowd, having gone to bed, for they had to rise early, to guard the gates of the deserted kingdom.

THE MAN of flesh, the man of passion, the man of thought. Lucas slept. His body, stripped to underclothes and half-covered with a sheet, submitted in oblivion to a harmony of forms. Gregg hopped and chirrupped on the lawn, dazzling himself with the illumination and talking aloud in his self-delight, though tomorrow he would be as cross as ever. Hook sat up with a start. The pillow and his horizontal position had been smothering him, and the phlegm in his throat could not be rasped away. His heart doubled its speed of beating; and gradually slowed. He moved his legs, blue bones in the cold light, to the floor and stood up in his nightshirt and walked about in his tiny room aimlessly. The moon so feeble previously now cast shadows through the window and rendered shapes: the bent boards of the little thick Bible, the open mouths of his shoes, the hang of his vest on the hook, the ribs of caning on the seat of his one chair. He opened his door and saw the blank bright green corridor wall across the way and closed it. His encounter with Conner had commenced to trouble him. The young man had been grievously stricken. The weakness on his face after his henchman had stolen the cigar was troubling to recall; an intimacy had been there Hook must reward with help. A small word would perhaps set things right. As a teacher, Hook's flaw had been over-conscientiousness; there was nowhere he would not meddle. He stood motionless, half in moonlight, groping after the fitful shadow of the advice he must impart to Conner, as a bond between them and a testament to endure his dying in the world. What was it?

A NOTE ON THE TYPE

THE TEXT of this book was set on the Linotype in Janson, a recutting made directly from type cast from matrices long thought to have been made by the Dutchman Anton Janson, who was a practicing type founder in Leipzig during the years 1668–87. However, it has been conclusively demonstrated that these types are actually the work of Nicholas Kis (1650–1702), a Hungarian, who most probably learned his trade from the master Dutch type founder Dirk Voskens. The type is an excellent example of the influential and sturdy Dutch types that prevailed in England up to the time William Caslon developed his own incomparable designs from them.

This book was printed and bound by
The Haddon Craftsmen, Scranton, Pennsylvania.